Florence Warden

A Witch of the Hills

Volume 2

Florence Warden

A Witch of the Hills
Volume 2

ISBN/EAN: 9783337391683

Printed in Europe, USA, Canada, Australia, Japan

Cover: Foto ©Andreas Hilbeck / pixelio.de

More available books at **www.hansebooks.com**

A

WITCH OF THE HILLS

BY

FLORENCE WARDEN

AUTHOR OF 'THE HOUSE ON THE MARSH,' ETC.

IN TWO VOLUMES

VOL. II

LONDON

RICHARD BENTLEY & SON, NEW BURLINGTON STREET

Publishers in Ordinary to Her Majesty the Queen

1888

A WITCH OF THE HILLS

CHAPTER XIV

THAT visit of Mr. Ellmer's,—hard as I tried,
and, as I believe, Babiole tried, to cheat myself into believing the contrary,—spoiled the
old frank intercourse between us for ever. It
was my fault, I know. Dreams that stirred
my soul and shook my body had sprung up
suddenly on that faint basis of a spurious tie
between me and the girl I had before half-
unconsciously loved. Now my long-torpid
passions stirred with life again and held Wal-
purgis Night revels within me. Our lessons

had to be laid by for a time, while I went
salmon-fishing, and tried to persuade myself
that it had been long neglect of my rod that
had caused forgotten passions and yearnings
to run riot in my blood in this undisciplined
manner. But it would not do. Tired out I
would drag my way home, eat a huge dinner,
and sink half-asleep into my old chair. Instead
of my falling into stupid, happy, dreamless
slumber, the leaden numbness of fatigue
would settle upon my limbs, while the one
figure whose growing ascendancy over my
whole nature I made these energetic efforts
to throw off, would pass and repass through
my mind's dull vision, the one thing distinct,
the one thing ever-recurring, enticing me to
follow it, eluding me, coming within my grasp,
escaping me, and so on for ever.

Then I tried a new tack : the lessons were
resumed. But we were both more reserved
than in the old days, and I, at least, was con-

strained also.   It was not the old child-pupil
sitting by my side ; it was the woman I wanted
to cherish in my bosom.   The old free cor-
rection, discussion, were exchanged for poor
endeavours by little implied compliments, by
mild attempts at eloquence, by appeals to her
sentiment when the subject in hand allowed
it, to gain her goodwill, to prepare her for the
time, which must come, when I should have
to entreat her to forget my hideous face and
try to love me as a husband.

I knew I was making hopeless, ridiculous
mistakes in my conduct towards her ; that the
change in my manner she took merely as an
acknowledgment that she was now in some
sort 'grown-up,' and answered by a little
added primness to show that she was equal
to the requirements of the new dignity.   I
felt that eight years' neglect of the sex threw
a man a century behind the times with regard
to his knowledge of women, and I was grow-

ing desperate when a ray of light came to me in the darkness of my clumsy courtship. I would consult Normanton, who was in the swim of the times, and who might be able to advise me as to the prudence of certain bold measures which, in my desperation, from time to time occurred to me. Neither Babiole nor I ever spoke about her father's visit, but the attempt to go on as if nothing had happened never grew any easier, and I welcomed the visit of my four friends, which took place rather earlier in the year than usual.

It was in the beginning of July that they all dropped in upon me in their usual casual fashion, and we had our first dinner together in a great tempest, excited by Edgar's announcement that this was his last bachelor holiday, as he was going to be married. I listened to the torrents of comment that, by long-standing agreement among us, were bound to be free, with new and painful in-

terest ; at any rate, I reflected that the private
advice I was going to ask of Edgar later
would now have the added weight of experience, and would, therefore, be more valuable
than it could have been in the old days of his
unregenerate contempt for women.   To hear
my Mentor browbeaten on this subject was
not altogether disagreeable to me, for I had
a keen memory of his somewhat lofty tone of
indulgence to me in the old times.

'And—er—what induced you to take this
step ?' asked Fabian, in an inquisitorial tone,
which implied the addition, 'without consult-
ing us.'   He was holding a glass of sherry in
his hand, and he looked at it as if he thought
that his friend's unaccountable conduct had
spoilt its flavour.

Edgar blushed and looked conscience-
stricken.   I feasted my eyes upon the sight.

'Well, I believe there is always a difficulty
about giving a satisfactory account of these

things,—an account, that is to say, which will satisfy the strict requirements of logic.'

'We expect an account consistent with your own principles, often and emphatically laid down. If you have not sinned against those, you will be listened to with indulgence,' said Fabian dogmatically. 'You shall be judged under your own laws.'

'Come, that's rather hard upon him,' pleaded Mr. Fussell.

Edgar dashed into his explanation in an off-hand manner.

'I met her at a tennis-party.' Maurice Browne, who hated muscular exercise, groaned. 'She was dressed in light blue flannel.' Fabian, who had been at Oxford, hissed. Edgar stopped to ask if this conduct were judicial.

'As a set-off against your advantage of being judged by your own laws, we claim the right to express our feelings each in his own manner,' explained Fabian. 'Go on.'

'We entered into conversation.' Dead but excited silence. 'I found she had read Browning,'—Murmurs of disgust from Fabian, of incredulity from Browne ; placid and vague murmur, implying ill-concealed non-apprehension, from Mr. Fussell,—'but did not understand him.' Explosion of mirth, in which everybody joined. 'I offered my services as some sort of interpreter.' Sardonic laugh from Browne. 'Merely on the assumption that a bad guess is better than none.' Interpellation from Fabian, ''Tis better to have guessed all wrong, than never to have guessed at all.' Edgar continued : 'After that we met again,'—deep attention,—'and again.' Murmurs of disappointment. 'At last we became engaged.'

A pause. Fabian drank a glass of champagne off hastily, and rose with frowns.

'It seems to me, gentlemen, that a taste for Browning and blue flannel, which is all our honourable friend seems to be able to put forward in favour of this lady, is a poor equipment for a person who (unless our honourable friend has gone back very far from his often-declared views on the subject of matrimony) is to be his guiding genius to political glory, the spur to his languid ambition, the beacon to his best aspirations,—in fact, gentlemen, the tug-boat to his man-of-war.'

'And as no girl reads Browning except under strong masculine pressure,' added Browne gravely, 'our friend the man-of-war must make up his mind that other and perhaps handsomer vessels have been towed before him, with the same rope.'

'Is the lady handsome?' asked Mr. Fussell.

Edgar hesitated. 'She has an intelligent face,' he said.

Upon this there arose much diversity of opinion; Fabian holding that this was consistent and even praiseworthy, while Maurice Browne and Mr. Fussell agreed that to deliberately marry a woman without positive and incontestable beauty ought to disqualify a man for the franchise as a person unfit for any exercise of judgment. When, however, Edgar, after allowing the controversy to rage, quietly produced and passed round the portrait of a girl beautiful enough to convert the sternest bachelor, there was a great calm, and the conversation, with a marked change of current, flowed smoothly into the abstract question of marriage. Edgar was not only acquitted ; he changed places with his judges. Every objection to matrimony was put forward in apologetic tones.

'For my part, when I speak bitterly of marriage, of course I am prejudiced by my own experience,' said Mr. Fussell, with a sigh that was jolly in spite of himself. He was separated from his wife,—everybody knew that; but he ignored—perhaps even scarcely took in the significance of—the fact that he had previously deserted her again and again.

Maurice Browne averred that his only objection to marriage was that it was an irrational bond; men and women, being animals with the disadvantage of speech to confuse each other's reason, should, like the other animals, be free to take a fresh partner every year.

This was received in silence, none of us being strong enough in natural history to contradict him, though we had doubts. He added that a book of his which was shortly to be brought out would, he thought, do much to bring about a more logical view of this matter, and to do away with the present vicious, because unnatural, restrictions.

Mr. Fussell, the person present whose private conduct would the least bear close inspection, was sincerely shocked, and wished to speak in the interests of morality, when

Fabian broke in, too full of his own views to bear discussion of other people's.

'Marriage,' he asserted in his excitable manner, 'for princes, for dukes, for grocers, and, in fact, the general rabble of humanity, is not a choice, but a necessity, according to the present state of things, which I see no pressing need to alter. But for the chosen ones of the earth—the artists,'—involuntarily I thought of Mr. Ellmer,—'by which I, of course, mean all those who, animated by some spark of the divine fire, have obeyed the call of Art, and given their lives and energies to her in one or another of her highest forms,— for us artists, I say, marriage is so much an impediment, so much an impossibility, that I unhesitatingly brand as mock-artists those fiddlers, mummers, and paint-smudgers who prefer the vulgar joys of domestic union to the savage independence and isolation which Art—true Art—imperatively demands. The wife of an artist—for as long as the pure soul of an artist remains weighted by a gross and exacting body, as long as he has dinners to be cooked, shirt-buttons to be sewn on, and desires to be satisfied, he may have what the world calls a wife ; that wife must be content with the position of a kindly-treated slave.'

At this point there arose a tumult, and somebody threw a cork at him. He wanted to say more, but even Browne, who had given him a little qualified applause, desired to hear no more ; and amid kindly assurances that hanging was too good for him, and that it was to be hoped Art would make it hot for him, and so forth, he sat down, and I, perceiving that we were all growing rather warm over this subject, suggested a move to the drawing-room, into which I had had the piano taken.

A little figure in pale pink stuff sprang up from a seat in the corner as we came in, let-

ting a big volume of old-fashioned engravings
fall from her arms. It was Babiole, who had
been too deep in her discovery of a new book
to expect us so soon. She gave a quick
glance at the window by which she had prepared a way of escape ; but seeing that it was
too late, she came forward a few steps without
confusion and held out her hand to Fabian,
who seemed much struck with the improve-
ment two years had brought about in her
appearance. Then, after receiving the greet-
ings of the rest, she excused herself on the
plea that her mother was waiting for her at
tea, and made a bow, in which most of us saw
a good deal of grace, to Maurice Browne,
who held open the door for her.

As Browne then made a rush to the piano,
I lost no time in taking Edgar on one side
under pretence of showing him an article in a
review, and in unburdening myself to him
with very little preface. I was in love, hope-

lessly in love. He guessed with whom at once, but did not understand my difficulty.

'She seems a modest, intelligent little girl ; she has every reason to be grateful to you, even fond of you. Why should you be so diffident ? '

I explained that she was beautiful, romantic, inexperienced ; that her head was still full of silky-locked princes and moated castles, or with creatures of her fancy little less impossible ; all sorts of dream-passions were seething in her girl's brain I knew, for I understood the little creature with desperate clearness of vision which only seemed to make her more inaccessible to me. If I could only conquer that terrible diffidence, that overwhelming awe that her fairy-like ignorance and innocence of the realities of life imposed upon me, I felt that I could plead my cause with a fire and force that would surmount even that ghastly obstacle of my hideous face ; but then, again, fire and force were no weapons to use against the indifference of childlike innocence; and to ask her in cold blood to marry me without making her heart speak first in my favour would be monstrous.   She had looked upon me till lately as she would have looked upon her grandfather, and this unsatisfactory affection had given place lately to a reserve which was even more unpromising.   Edgar listened to me, did not deny the enormous fascination of a young mind one has one's self helped to form, but thought that I should resist it, and was rather indignant that I had not taken the opportunity of her father's visit to rid myself of mother and daughter to-gether.   He inclined to the idea that the two unlucky women were imposing on my gener-osity and were determined to make 'a good thing' out of me, and it was not until I had spent some time in explaining minutely the footing upon which we stood to one another that his prejudices began to give way.

At this point I perceived that Maurice Browne was playing at chess with Mr. Fussell, while Fabian had disappeared. When the game was over, they insisted on our joining them at whist. Before we had played one game I began to grow nervous at Fabian's long absence, and Mr. Fussell, who was my partner, took to leaning over the table as soon as I put down a card, and with one finger fixed viciously in the green cloth, and his starting eyes peering up into my face over his double eyeglass, saying in a sepulchral voice—

'*Did* you see what was played, Mr. Maude?'

I had trumped his trick, revoked, and done everything else that I ought not to have done before the missing Fabian came back in a tornado of high spirits, and with a tiny white

Scotch rose at his buttonhole. Now there was only one Scotch rose-bush in the garden, and it grew by the porch of the cottage and was Babiole's private property. When the hand was played out I got Fabian to take my place, for my fingers shook so that I could not sort my cards.

While I had been arguing with Edgar the necessity of delicacy in making love to a young girl, Fabian had dashed into the breach, and now bore the trophy of a first success on his breast.

CHAPTER XV

I BELIEVE that Edgar, in the innocence of his heart, thought that Fabian's headlong flirtation and flaunting success with the girl I loved in such meek and forlorn fashion formed a salutary experience for me.

For while the young actor invariably sloped from fishing excursions, and disappeared from picnics, and had a flower which I absolutely recognised in his buttonhole every day, Edgar contented himself with preaching to me a philosophical calm, and ignored my pathetic insinuations that he might do some unspecified good by 'speaking to' Fabian. Indeed, that would have been

a delicate business; especially as I had an-
nounced myself to be the girl's guardian, and
she was thus undeniably well provided with
protectors. All the consolation I had was the
reflection that this flirtation could only last a
fortnight; but as it was my guests themselves
who fixed not only the date but the duration
of their stay, even this comfort was destroyed
by their agreeing among themselves to extend
their visit by another ten days. When I
learned that this was upon the proposal of
Fabian I took a stern resolution. I invited
Mrs. Ellmer and her daughter to join us in
all our expeditions, so as to establish an effec-
tive check upon the freedom of their intercourse. The result of this was that Mrs.
Ellmer abandoned herself to a rattling flirtation with Mr. Fussell, while Fabian walked off
with Babiole to gather flowers, or to climb hills,
or to race Ta-ta, in the most open manner, and
Edgar laughed at my annoyance, and talked

about hens and ducklings to me in an exasperating undertone.

I think he began to believe that I was
entering prematurely into the doddering and
senile stage—this straight, wholesome, handsome fellow, who disdained the least pang of
jealousy of the girl who was fortunate enough
to have secured his magnanimous approval.
If he had been branded with a disfiguring
scar, he would have renounced the joys of
love with such staunch, heroic, 'broad-shoul-
dered' fortitude, that there would have been
quite a rush for the honour of consoling him ;
it was not in him to find anything deeper
than lip-compassion for feverish and morbid
emotions. I admired his grand and healthy
obtuseness, and wished that he could bind
my eyes too. But I saw plainly enough the
radiance of unnatural exaltation of feeling
which lighted up the young girl's face after
a walk with Fabian, and I knew that the

hectic enthusiasm of his artist temperament was kindling fires in the sensitive nature, which it would be danger to feed and ruin to extinguish. With a morbid sensibility of which I was ashamed, I could look into the girl's glowing blue eyes as I shook her hand and bade her good-night, and feel in my own soul every emotion that had stirred her heart as she roamed over the hills with Fabian that day.

It was near the end of the third week of my visitors' stay, that I waited one night for Fabian's return from the cottage, to which he and Mr. Fussell had escorted the two ladies, who had dined with us. Mr. Fussell had returned, and gone into the house to play cards. Fabian came back sixteen minutes later. There had been a proposal to extend my visitors' stay still further, and upon that hint I had determined to speak. I was leaning against the portico, as we called the porch of the house, to distinguish it from that of the cottage. I had smoked through two cigars while I was waiting, but at the sound of his footsteps I threw the third away. Fabian walked with a long swinging step: off the stage the man was too earnest to saunter; crossing a room, eating his breakfast, always seemed a matter of life or death to him; and if he had to call a second time for his shaving-water, it was in the tones of a Huguenot while the Saint Bartholomew was at its height. I had always looked upon him as a very good fellow, impetuous but honour-able, doing intentional harm to no one. But I knew the elasticity of my sex's morality where nothing stronger than the sentiments is concerned, and I knew that his impetuosity was kept in some sort of check by his ambition. His restless erratic life, and his avowed principles, were antagonistic to happy marriage, and I knew that he was in the habit of satisfying the *besoin d'aimer* by open and chivalrous attachments to now one and now another distinguished lady ; and this knightly devotion to Queens of Love and Beauty, though it makes very pretty reading in the chronicles of the Middle Ages, is not, in the interest of nineteenth century domestic peace, a thing to be revived. So, although I had miserable doubts that the steed was already stolen, I was determined to lock the stable door.

'Lovely night,' said he. 'I like your Scotch hills at night ; and, for the matter of that, I like them in the daytime too.'

Fabian always sank the fact that he was a Scotchman, though I burned just now with the conviction that he was tainted with the national hypocrisy.

'I suppose you will be glad to get back to the hum and roar again by this time, though,' I said as carelessly as I could.

Fabian had none of Edgar's serene obtuseness. He looked at me to find out what I meant.

'Well, you know, we were thinking of imposing ourselves upon you for another week, if you have no objection.'

This show of civility was the first shadow on our unceremonious intercourse. In spite of myself I was this evening grave and stiff, and not to be approached with the customary affectionate familiarity. There was silence while one might have counted twenty. Then I said—

'That was *your* proposal, was it not?'

I spoke so gravely, so humbly, that my question, rude as it was in itself, could not offend.

'Why—yes,' said he in a tone as low and as serious as my own. 'What's the matter, Harry?'

'Will you tell me, honestly, why you want to stay?'

His big burning eyes looked intently into my face, and then he put one long thin hand through his hair and laughed.

'Well, after all that you've done to make our stay agreeable, that's a queer question to ask.'

I put my hand on his shoulder and forced him to keep still.

'Look here, Faby, I don't want to insult you, you know; but are you staying because of that little girl?'

He drew himself up and answered me with a very fine and knightly fire—

'Do you take me for a scoundrel?'

'No; if I did you would never have touched the child's hand.'

'Then what do you mean?'

'Simply this, that I know Babiole better than you do, and I can see that every word you say to her strikes down deeper than you think. She is an imaginative little—fool if you like ; she believes that the romance of her life is come, and she is beginning to live upon it and upon nothing else.'

Fabian considered, looking down upon the grass, in which he was digging a deep symmetrical hole with his right heel. At last he looked up.

'I think you're wrong ; I do indeed,' he said earnestly. 'You know as well as I do that my trotting about with her has always been as open as the day ; that it was taken for granted there was no question of serious love-making with a mere child like that. I'm sure her mother never thought of such a thing for a moment.'

Now I knew that Mrs. Ellmer, on principle, scoffed so keenly at love in her daughter's presence, by way of wholesome repression of the emotions, that she would be sure to think that she had scoffed away all danger of its inopportune appearance.

'My dear boy, I acquit you of all blame in the matter. The mother we can leave out of account; she is not a person of the most delicate discrimination. But I tell you I have watched the girl——'

'That is enough,' interrupted Fabian abruptly, and with off-hand haughtiness. 'Of course, if I had understood that you were personally interested in the little girl——'

I interrupted in my turn. 'I am interested only in getting her well, that is—happily—married.'

Fabian bowed. 'You are anticipating your troubles with your ward, or pupil, or whatever you call her,' said he lightly, though he was angry enough for his words to have a bitter tone. 'However, of course I respect your solicitude, and Babiole and I must, for the next few days, hunt butterflies on separate hills.'

And shaking me by the shoulder, and

laughing at me for an old woman, he went into the house.

But he was obstinate, or more interested than he pretended to be. I know that it was he who next morning at breakfast put up Fussell and Maurice Browne to great eagerness for the extension of their stay. When I regretted that I had made arrangements for going to Edinburgh on business on the date already settled for their departure, Fabian glanced up at my face with a vindictive expression which startled me.

This was the last day but one of my visitors' stay. We all went on the coach to Braemar, having taken our places the night before. As we all walked in the early morning to Ballater station, from which the coach starts, I overheard Fabian say to Babiole—

'We shan't be able to see much of each other to-day, little one. Your maiden aunt disapproves of my picking flowers for you.

But I'll get as near as I can to you on the coach, and this evening you must get mamma to invite me to tea.'

'Maiden aunt!' she repeated, evidently not understanding him.

They were behind me, so that I could not see their faces; but by a glance, a gesture, or a whisper Fabian must have indicated me; for she burst out—

'Oh, you must not laugh at him; it is not right; I won't hear anything against Mr. Maude.'

'Sh! Against him! Oh dear, no!' And the sneer died away in words I could not hear.

They had fallen back, I suppose, for I lost even the sound of their voices; but I heard no more than before of the monologue on the New Era in literature to which Maurice Browne was treating me. He was the pioneer of this New Era, so we understood;

and there was so much more about the pioneer than about the era in his talk on this his favourite subject, that we, who were quite satisfied to know no more of the inmost workings of his mind than was revealed by the small talk of daily existence, seldom gave him a chance of unburdening himself fully except when our minds, like mine on this occasion, were deeply engaged with other matters.

On the coach Fabian sat next to Babiole, who looked so sweet in a white muslin hat and a frock made of the stuff with which drawing-room chairs are covered up when the family are out of town, that Maurice Browne, in a burst of enthusiasm, compared her to a young brown and white rabbit. Fabian had brought his umbrella, so I told myself, for the express purpose of holding it over his companion in such a manner as to prevent me, on the back seat, from seeing the ardent gaze of the man, the shy glances of the girl, which I jealously imagined underneath. Everybody declared that it was a beautiful drive; I had thought so myself a good many times before. The winding Dee burnt its way through the valley in a blaze of sunlight on our left, past the picturesque little tower of Abergeldie, with its rough walls and corner turret; past stately, romantic Balmoral, whose white pinnacles and battlements peeped out, with royal and appropriate reserve, from behind a screen of trees, on the other side of the river, far below us. Near here we found our fresh team, standing quietly under a tree, by a ruined and roofless stone building. Oddly frequent they are, these ruinous farms and cottages, in the royal neighbourhood. As we drew near Braemar the scenery grew wilder and grander. Between the peaks of the bare steep hills, where little patches of

tall fir-trees grow on inaccessible ledges on
the face of the dark-gray rock, we caught
glimpses of Lochnagar, with its snow-cap
dwindled by the summer sun into thin white
lines. We passed close under steep Craig
Clunie, where the story goes that Colonel
Farquharson, of Clunie, hid himself after
the battle of Culloden, and heard King
George's soldiers making merry over their
victory in his mansion, which, in common
with all old Scotch country-houses, is called
a castle. As the castle is three-quarters of a
mile from the Craig, Edgar opined that the
Colonel must have had sharp ears. Then
he scoffed a little at the obstinate ignorance
of the Highland gentlemen who would
hazard an acre in defence of such a futile
and worthless person as Charles James
Stuart. Edgar had advanced political
notions, which, in another man, I should
have called rabid. I said that if it had been

merely a matter of persons, and not of principles, I should have backed up the Colonel, since I would sooner swear allegiance to a home-born profligate than to one of foreign growth ; but then I own I would have English princes marry English ladies, and I feel a sneaking regard for Henry the Eighth for having given his countrywomen a chance, and thereby left to the world our last great sovereign by right of birth, Queen Elizabeth.

That umbrella in front of me had made me cantankerous, I daresay ; at any rate, I disagreed persistently with Edgar for the rest of the way, and called Old Mar Castle a mouldy old rat-hole merely because he was struck with admiration of its many-turreted walls. We had luncheon at the Fife Arms, where we were all overpowered by Mr. Fussell, who, having been allowed by the coachman to drive for about half a mile as we came, became so puffed up by his superiority, and so tiresomely loud in his boasts about his driving that, Fabian being too much occupied with Babiole to shut him up, and nobody else having the requisite dash and disregard of other people's feelings, we all sneaked away from the table, one by one, as quickly as we could, and left him to finish by himself the champagne he had ordered. These three, therefore, spent the hours before our return in the neighbourhood of Braemar together. While keeping within the letter of his promise to have no more *tête-à-tête* walks with Babiole, Fabian thus easily violated the spirit of it; since Mr. Fussell, being too stout and too sleepy after luncheon to do much walking, suggested frequent and long rests under the trees, which he spent with gently-clasped hands, and a handerchief over his face to keep the flies off.

The rest of us took a beastly hot walk to the Falls of Corriemulzie, and I wondered what I could have before seen to admire in them. Coming back, Mrs. Ellmer chased Maurice Browne for some indiscreet compliment. A tropical sun would not have taken the vivacity out of that woman! and Edgar fell through a fence on which he was resting, was planted in a bramble, and said 'Damn' for the first recorded time in the presence of a lady. That is all I remember of the expedition.

For the return journey, as Mr. Fussell had retired into the interior of the coach for a nap, being the laziest of men when he was not the busiest, I took the box-seat by the coachman, and was thus spared the sight of another *tête-à-tête*. After dinner that evening Fabian disappeared as usual in the direction of the cottage, and on the following day, which was the last of my visitors' stay, he

threw his promise to the winds so openly that
I began to think he must have made up his
mind to let his principles go by the board, and
make love seriously.   In that case, of course,
I could have nothing to say, and however
much I might choose to torment myself with
doubts as to the permanent happiness of the
union, I had really no grounds for believing
that his vaunted principles would stand the
test of practical experience better than did
the ante-matrimonial prattle of more commonplace young men.

On the morning of my guests' departure
the house was all astir at five o'clock in the
morning.   There was really no need for this
effort, as the train did not leave Ballater till
8.25, and my Norfolk cart and a fly from
M'Gregor's would not be at the door before
half-past seven.   But it was a convention
among us to behave to the end like school-
boys, and, after all, a summer sunrise among

the hills is a thing to be seen once and remembered for ever.

So there was much running up and down
stairs, and sorting of rugs and collecting of
miscellaneous trifles (I declare if they had
been professional pickpockets I could not
have dreaded more the ravages they made
among the more modern and spicy of the
volumes in my library), and there was a
general disposition to fall foul of Edgar for
the approaching vagary of his marriage,
which would break up our Round Table
hopelessly.

' I look upon this as a " long, a last good-
bye " to Normanton,' said Maurice Browne,
shaking his head. ' No man passes through
the furnace of matrimony unchanged. When
we see him again he may be a *better* man,
refined by trial, ennobled by endurance ; but
he will not be the *same*. He will be a phœnix
risen from the ashes of the old——'

'Or a wreck broken up by the waves,' added Mr. Fussell.

I looked out of one of the eastern windows at the red sun-glow, in which I took more pleasure than the Londoners, perhaps because I considered it as a part of my Highland property. To the left, standing in the long wet grass, shyly hiding herself among the trees, was Babiole ; I went to another window from which I could see her more plainly, and discovered that her little face was much paler than usual, that she was watching the portico with straining eyes ; in her hand, but held behind her, was a red rose, that she drew out from time to time and even kissed. I think she was crying. It was half-past six o'clock. I turned away and went back to my friends, who were already deep in a gigantic breakfast. From time to time I went back, on some pretext or other, to the window : she was always there, in the same place. The

fourth time I looked out she was shivering;
and her hands, red with the cold of the morning, were tucked up to her throat, red rose
and all. I went up to Fabian, who I am
sure must have been at quite his third chop,
and touched him on the shoulder.

'There's some one waiting outside,—waiting for you, I think,' said I, in a low voice,
under cover of the rich full tones of my true
friend Fussell, who was waxing warm in the
eloquence of his farewell to Scotch breakfasts.

Fabian got up at once and went out. I saw
the child start forward, crimson in a moment,
and the tears flowing undisguisedly; and with
a choking feeling at my throat I turned away.

'Hallo, why you're not eating, Harry,'
cried Maurice presently. 'You must be in
love.'

'Another of 'em!' groaned Fussell.

'No,' said I hastily. 'The fact is I had
something to eat before you came down.'

There was a roar at my voracity, but their own appetites were too vigorous for them to disbelieve me.   I remember clearly only this of our final departure for the station : that Fabian turned up late, dashing after us down the drive in fact, and leaping up on to the Norfolk cart beside me.   And that his eyes were dry, but that the front of his coat, just below the collar, was wet, perhaps with the dew.   Nevertheless, if Edgar had not been behind us, I should have felt much inclined, when we drove along the road by the Dee, just where the bank is nice and steep, to give a jerk of the reins to the left, pitch my artistic friend out into the river's stony bed, and take my risk of following him.

CHAPTER XVI

LIFE seemed to move in a somewhat slow and stagnant manner for several days after the departure of my guests. I scarcely saw Babiole, and never spoke to her, a great shyness towards each other having taken possession of both of us. Mrs. Ellmer, upon whom I made a ceremonious call when I could contain my anxious interest no longer, was stiff in manner, haughty and depressed. She had evidently been informed of my opposition to Fabian's intention of extending his stay, and I soon learnt, to my great surprise, that she considered me responsible for the destruction of Babiole's first chance—

'and the only one she is likely to have, poor child, living poked up here,' of 'settling well.'

'Oh,' said I, raising my eyebrows, and putting into that one exclamation as much sardonic emphasis as I could, while I kept my eyes fixed upon the cat and my hands much occupied with my deer-stalker, 'and may I be permitted to learn how I have done this ?'

'It is useless to put on a satirical manner with me, Mr. Maude,' said the lady with dignity ; 'I am perfectly aware that it was you who objected to Mr. Scott's remaining here long enough to make proposals for my daughter, and that, in fact, you interfered in the most marked way with his courtship of her.'

'And are you ignorant of the fact, madam, that to interfere with a man's courtship is the very way to increase its warmth, and that if my interference, as you call it, could not screw him up to the point of proposing, nothing ever would ?'

Mrs. Ellmer dropped into her lap the work which she had snatched up on my entrance, and at which she had been stitching away ever since, as a hint that she was busy and would be glad to be left alone ; at the same time being, I think, not sorry to vent her ill-humour on some one.

'You are using very extraordinary expressions, Mr. Maude,' she said acidly. ' If her mother was satisfied with the gentleman's behaviour, I really don't see what business you had in the affair at all.'

' Do you forget that her father has made me responsible for the care of her ? that she is certainly under my guardianship, and nominally engaged to me.'

' Nominally ! There it is. To be engaged to a man who acknowledges that he never

means to marry you! There's a pretty
position for a girl, as I've said to Babiole
scores of times!'

My heart leaped up.

'You've said that to Babiole!' I echoed,
in a voice of suppressed rage that brought
the little slender virago at once to reason.

'Well, Mr. Maude, with all respect to you,
the position is something like that,' she said
more reasonably.

'It is not at all like that,' I answered in
my gravest and most magisterial tones. 'If
your daughter could by any possibility overcome a young girl's natural repugnance to
take for husband such an unsightly object as
accident has made me, I should be a much
happier man than I am ever likely to be.
But she could not do so; there is such a
ghastly incongruity about a marriage of
that sort that I could scarcely even wish
her to do so.'

Mrs. Ellmer's eyes had begun to glow with the carefully but scarcely successfully subdued interest of the match-making mamma. This, however, gave place to uneasy disappointment as I went on—

'All the same I take an interest in your daughter's happiness quite as strong as if it were a more selfish one. It was that interest which prompted me to prevent the prolonging of a flirtation which might have serious consequences for your sensitive and impressionable little daughter.'

'Serious consequences!' stammered Mrs. Ellmer. 'Do you mean to say that Mr. Scott, your friend, is a dishonourable man?'

'No,' said I, 'I would not say anything so severe as that. But I am certainly of opinion that Mr. Scott had no more serious intention than to fill up his time here pleasantly by talks and walks with a pretty and charming girl. Lots of pretty and charming

girls accept such temporary devotion for
what it is worth, and their regrets, when the
amusement is over, are proportionately light.
But I know that Babiole is not like that, and
so I did all that my limited powers of
guardianship could do to lessen the danger.'

'But he may still write and propose,'
murmured the dismayed mother. 'Even if
his intentions were not serious while he was
here, he may find he cannot get on without
her!'

I wanted to shake the woman, or to box
her ears, and ask her how she had dared
wittingly to expose her daughter to the misery
of hanging on to such a hope as this.

'I don't think it's likely,' I said drily; and
questioning my face with doubt in her eyes,
the match-maker tried another tack.

'After all, Mr. Maude, it may be for the
best,' she began in a conciliatory tone. 'It
was I, rather than Babiole, that was so hot

upon this match, not understanding that my
poor child had any chance of a better husband.
For my part, I don't see that you have
any reason to talk about yourself in the dis-
ponding manner you do, and if you will only
trust for a little while to my diplomacy, and
speak to her when I give you the word that
it's the right moment——'

I interrupted her by standing up suddenly,
and I can only hope my face did not express
what I thought of her and her miserable
diplomacy.

'You will oblige me by saying not one
word to your daughter on the subject of me
and my impossible pretensions,' I said authoritatively, but with a sickening knowledge
that my demand would be disregarded. 'I
am sensitive enough and humble enough on
the score of my own disadvantages, I admit.
But I am not a miserable wreck of humanity
who would take what perfunctory favours a

woman would throw to him, and be satisfied. I am a man with powers of loving that any woman might be proud to excite; and no girl shall ever be my wife who does not feel of her own accord, and show, as an innocent girl can, that I have done her a honour in loving her which she is bound to pay back by loving me with all her might.'

And much excited by my own unexpected burst of unreserve, but somewhat ashamed of having rather bullied a poor creature who, however she might assume the high hand with me, was after all but an unprotected and plucky little woman, I held out my hand with apologetic meekness and prepared to go. Mrs. Ellmer shook my hand limply and showed a disposition to whimper.

'Don't worry yourself and don't bother— I mean—er—don't talk to the child.   It will come all right.   She's hardly grown up yet; there's plenty of time for half-a-dozen princely suitors to turn up. And what do you say to taking her once a week to Aberdeen and giving her some good music lessons? It will distract her thoughts a bit, and do you both good.'

This suggestion diverted the little woman's tears, and her face softened with a kindly impulse towards me.

'You are very good, Mr. Maude, you really are,' she said in farewell as I left her.

And though I was grateful for this *amende*, I should have been more pleased if I could have felt assured that she would not, in default of Mr. Scott, tease her daughter with recommendations to get used to the idea of myself in the capacity of lover.

Of course after this interview I was more shy than ever of meeting Babiole, and even when, on the second evening afterwards, I saw her standing in the rose garden, appar-

ently waiting for me to come and speak to
her, I pretended not to see her, and after
examining the sky as if to make out the signs
by which one might predict the weather of
the morrow, I turned back to finish my cigar
in the drive.   But the evening after that
I found on my table a great bowl full of
flowers from her own private garden, and on
the following afternoon, while I was writing
a letter, there came pattering little steps in
the hall and a knock at my open study door.

'Come in,' said I, feeling that I had gone
purple and that the thumping of my heart
must sound as loudly as a traction engine in
the road outside.

Babiole came in very quietly, with a
bright flush on her face and shy eyes.   Her
hands were full of tiny wild flowers, and
among them was one little sprig carefully
tied up with ribbon.

'I found a plant of white heather this

morning on one of the hills by the side of
the Gairn,' said she quickly. 'You know
they say it is so rare that some Highlanders
never see any all their lives. It brings luck
they say.'

'Why do you bring it to me then?' I
asked, as she put the little blossom on the
table beside me. 'You should keep luck for
yourself, and not waste it on a person who
doesn't deserve any.'

She had nothing to say to this, so she
only gave the flower a little push towards me
to intimate that I was to enter into possession
without delay. I took it up and stuck it in
the buttonhole of my old coat.

'It has brought me luck already, you see,
since this is the first visit I have had from
you for I don't know how long,' I said, looking up at her, and noticing at once with a
pang that she had grown in ten days paler
and altogether less radiant.

She blushed deeply at this, and sliding down on to her knees, put her arms round Ta-ta, and kissed the collie's ears.

'Ta-ta has missed you awfully,' I went on; 'she told me yesterday that you never take her out on the hills now, and that her digestion is suffering in consequence. She says her tail is losing all its old grand sweep for want of change of air.'

Babiole smoothed the dog's coat affectionately.

'I haven't been out much lately,' she said in a low voice; 'there has been a great deal to do in the cottage, and here too. I've been hemming some curtains for Janet, and helping mamma to make pickles. Oh, I've been very busy, indeed.'

'And I suppose all this amazing superabundance of work is over at last, since you can find time to come and pay calls of ceremony on chance acquaintances.'

She looked up at me reproachfully. My spirits had been rising ever since she came in, and I would only laugh at her.

'I'm sure it is quite time those curtains were hemmed and those pickles were made, so that you can have a chance to go back to Craigendarroch and look about for those roses you've left there.'

'Roses! Oh, do I look white then?' And she began to rub her cheeks with her hands to hide the blush that rose to them.

'Has your mother said anything to you about Aberdeen and the music lessons?'

'Yes.' She looked up with a loving smile.

I had turned my chair round to the fireplace, where a little glimmer of fire was burning; for it was a wet cool day. Babiole had seated herself on a high cloth-covered footstool, and Ta-ta sat between us, looking from the one to the other and wagging her tail to

congratulate us on our return to the old terms
of friendship. The sky outside was growing
lighter towards evening, and the sun was
peeping out in a tearful and shamefaced way
from behind the rain-clouds. The girl and
the sun together had made a great illumina-
tion in the old study, though they were not
at their brightest.

'Well, and how do you like the idea?'

'It is quite perfect, like all your ideas for
making other people happy.'

'I'm afraid I don't always succeed very
well.'

This she took as a direct accusation, and
she bent her head very low away from me.

'Has your mother been talking to you,
Babiole?'

'Yes'—as a guilty admission.

'What did she say?'

'Oh, she talked and talked. That was
why I didn't like to come and see you. You

see, though I told her she didn't understand, and that whatever you thought must
be right, yet hearing all those things made
me feel that I—I couldn't come in the old
way. And then at last I missed you so—
that I thought I would dash in and—get it
over.'

From which I gathered that Mrs. Ellmer
had babbled out the whole substance of our
interview, and coloured it according to her
lights, so I ventured—

'Didn't you feel at all angry with me for
something I said—something I did?'

A pause. I could see nothing of her face,
for she was most intent upon making a beau-
tifully straight parting with my ink-stained
old ivory paper-knife down the back of
Ta-ta's head.

'I had no right to be angry,' she said at
last, in a quivering voice, 'and besides—I am
afraid—that what you said will come true.'

And the tears began to fall upon her busy fingers. I put my hand very gently upon her brown hair and could feel the thrill sent through her whole frame by a valiant struggle to repress an outburst of grief.

'You are afraid then that——' And I waited.

'That he will never think of me again,' she sobbed; and unable any longer to repress her feelings, she sat at my feet for some minutes quietly crying.

I hoped that the distress which could find this childlike outlet would be only a transient one, and I thought it best for her to let her tears flow unrestrainedly, as I was sure she had no chance of doing under the sharp maternal eyes. I continued to smooth her hair sympathetically until by a great effort she conquered herself and dried her eyes.

'I am a great baby,' she said indignantly; 'as if I could hope that a very clever accom-

plished man, whom all the world is talking
about, would be able to remember an
ignorant girl like me, when once he had
got back to London.'

'Well, and you must pull yourself together and forget him,' I said—I hope not
savagely.

But there came a great change over her
face, and she said almost solemnly—

'No, I don't want to do that—even if I
could. I want to remember all he told me
about art, and about ideals, and to become
an accomplished woman, so that I may meet
him some day, and he may be quite proud
that it was he who inspired me.'

So Mr. Scott had known how, by a little
dash and plausibility, and by deliberately
playing upon her emotions, to crown my
work and to appropriate to himself the credit
and the reward of it all.

But after this enthusiastic declaration

the light faded again out of her sensitive face.

'It seems such a long, long time to wait before that can happen,' she said mournfully.

And a remarkably poor ambition to live upon, I thought to myself.

'And do you think Mr. Scott's approbation is worth troubling your head about if, after all his enthusiasm about you, he forgets you as soon as you are out of his sight?' I asked rather bitterly.

Cut at this suggestion, corresponding so exactly with her own fears, she almost broke down again. It was in a broken voice that she answered—

'I can't think hardly about him; when I do it only makes me break my heart afterwards, and I long to see him to ask his pardon for being so harsh. He was fond of me while he was here, I couldn't expect more

than that of such a clever man.   And he has
sent me one letter—and perhaps—I hope—
he will send me another before long.'

'He has written to you?'

'Yes.'   As a mark of deep friendship for
me she not only let me see the envelope
(preserved in a black satin case embroidered
with pink silk) but flourished before my eyes
the precious letter itself, a mere scrap of a
note, I could see that, and not the ten-pager
of your disconsolate lover.

I was seized with a great throb of impatience, and clave the top coal of the small
fire viciously.   She must get over this.   I
turned the subject, for fear I should wound
her feelings by some outburst of anger
against Mr. Scott, who must indeed have
worked sedulously to leave such a deep
impression on the girl's mind.

'Well, you will have to be content with
your old master's affection for the present,

Babiole,' I said, when she had put her treasure carefully away.

'Oh, Mr. Maude!' She leant lovingly against my knee.

'And if the worst comes to the worst you will have to marry me.'

She laughed as if this were a joke in my best manner.

'Didn't your mother say anything to you about that?' I asked, as if carrying on the jest.

Babiole blushed. 'Don't talk about it,' she said humbly. 'I lost my temper, and spoke disrespectfully to her for the first time. I told her she ought to be ashamed of herself, after all you have done for us.'

Evidently she thought the idea originated with her mother, and was pressed upon me against my inclination. Seeing that I should gain nothing by undeceiving her, I laughed the matter off, and we drifted into a talk about the garden, and the croup among Mr. Blair's bare-footed children at the Mill o' Sterrin a mile away.

According to all precedent among love-lorn maidens, Babiole ought to have got over her love malady as a child gets over the measles, or else she ought to have dwindled into 'the mere shadow of her former self' and to have found a refined consolation in her beloved hills. But instead of following either of these courses, the little maid began to evince more and more the signs of a marked change, which showed itself chiefly in an inordinate thirst for work of every kind. She began by a renewed and feverish devotion to her studies with me, and assiduous practice on my piano whenever I was out, to get the fullest possible benefit from her music lessons at Aberdeen. This, I thought, was only the outcome of her ex-pressed desire to become an accomplished

woman.   But shortly afterwards she relieved
her mother of the whole care of the cottage,
filling up her rare intervals of time in helping
Janet.   Walks were given up, with the excep-
tion of a short duty-trot each day to Knock
Castle or the Mill o' Sterrin and back again.
When I remonstrated, telling her she would
lose her health, she answered restlessly—

'Oh, I hate walking, it is more tiring than
all the work—much more tiring!   And one
gets quite as much air in the garden as on
Craigendarroch, without catching cold.'

She was always perfectly sweet and good
with me, but she confessed to me sometimes,
with tears in her eyes, that she was growing
impatient and irritable with her mother.   I
had waited as eagerly as the girl herself for
another letter from Fabian Scott, but when
the hope of receiving one had died away, I
did not dare to say anything about the sore
subject.

About the middle of December she broke
down.   It was only a cold, she said, that
kept her in the cottage and even forced her
to lay aside all her incessant occupations.
But she had worked so much too hard lately
that she was not strong enough to throw it
off quickly, and day after day, when I went
to see her, I found my dear witch lying back
in the high wooden rocking-chair in the
sitting-room, with a very transparent-looking
skin, a poor little pink-tipped nose, and large,
luminous, sad eyes that had no business at all
in such a young face.

On the fifth day I was alone with her,
Mrs. Ellmer having fussed off to the
kitchen about dinner.   I was in a very
sentimental mood indeed, having missed my
little sunbeam frightfully.   Babiole had
pushed her rocking-chair quickly away from
the table, which was covered with a map and
a heap of old play-bills.   By the map lay a

pencil, which the girl had laid down on my entrance.

'What were you doing when I came in?' I asked, after a few questions about her health.

The colour came back for a moment to her face as she answered—

'I was tracing our old journeys together, mamma's and mine; and looking at those old play-bills with her name in them.'

The occupation seemed to me dismally suggestive.

'You were wishing you were travelling again, I suppose,' said I, in a tone which fear caused to sound hard.

'Oh no, at least not exactly,' said the poor child, not liking to confess the feverish longing for change and movement which had seized upon her like a disease.

I remained silent for a few minutes, struggling with hard facts, my hands clasped

together, my arms resting on my knees.
Then I said without moving, in a voice that
was husky in spite of all my efforts—

'Babiole, tell me, on your word of honour,
are you thinking about that man still?'

I could hear her breath coming in quick
sobs. Then she moved, and her fingers held
out something right under my averted eyes.
It was the one note she had received from
Fabian Scott, worn into four little pieces.

'Look here, dear,' I said, having signified
by a bend of the head that I understood,
'do you think a man like that would be likely
to make a good husband?'

'Oh no,' readily and sadly.

'But you would be his wife all the same?'

'Oh, Mr. Maude!' in a low trembling
voice, as if Paradise had been suddenly
thrown open to mortal sight.

I got up.

'Well, well,' I said, trying to speak in a

jesting tone, 'I suppose these things will be explained in a better world!'

Mrs. Ellmer came in at that moment, and the leave-taking for the day was easier.

'Won't you stay and lunch with us, Mr. Maude? I've just been preparing something nice for you,' she said with disappointment.

'Thank you, no, I can't stay this morning. The fact is I have to start for London this afternoon, and I haven't a minute to lose.'

Babiole started, and her eyes, as I turned to her to shake hands, shone like stars.

'Good-bye, Mr. Maude,' she faltered, taking my hand in both hers, and pressing it feverishly.

And she looked into my face without any inquiry in her gaze, but with a subdued hope and a boundless gratitude.

Mrs. Ellmer insisted on coming over to the house to see that everything was properly packed for me. As I left the cottage with her I looked back, and saw the little face, with its weird expression of eagerness, pressed against the window.

It was an awful thing I was going to do, certainly. But what sacrifice would not the worst of us make to preserve the creature we love best in the world from dying before our eyes?

CHAPTER XVII

I ARRIVED at King's Cross at 8.15 on the following morning, and after breakfasting at the Midland Hotel, went straight to Fabian Scott's chambers, in a street off the Haymarket. It was then a little after half-past ten.

Fabian, who was at breakfast, received me very heartily, and was grieved that I had not come direct to him.

'What would you have said,' he asked, 'if I had gone to have breakfast at the Invercauld Arms in Ballater, instead of coming on to you?'

'That's not quite the same thing, my

impetuous young friend. You didn't expect
me, for one thing, and London is a place
where one must be a little more careful of
one's behaviour than in the wilds.'

'No, that is true, I did not expect you;
though when I heard your name, I was so
pleased I thought I must have been living
on the expectation for the last month.'

'Out of sight, out of mind, according to
the simple old saying.'

I was looking about me, examining my
friend's surroundings, feeling discouraged by
the portraits of beautiful women, photographs
on the mantelpiece, paintings on the walls,
the invitation cards stuck in the looking-
glass, the crested envelopes, freshly torn, on
the table; the room, which seemed effem-
inately luxurious, after my sombre, threadbare,
old study, gave no evidence of bachelor
desolation. It was just untidy enough to
prove that 'when a man's single he lives at

his ease,' for an opera hat and a soiled glove
lay on the chair, a new French picture, which
a wife would have tabooed, was propped up
against the back of another, and on the
mantelpiece was a royal disorder, in which a
couple of pink clay statuettes of pierrettes,
by Van der Straeten, showed their piquant,
high-hatted little heads, and their befrilled,
high-lifted little skirts above letters, ash
trays, cigarette cases, 'parts' in MS.,
sketches, a white tie, a woman's long glove,
the 'proof' of an article on 'The Cathedrals
of Spain,' and a heap of other things. In
the centre stood a handsome Chippendale
clock, surmounted by signed photographs of
Sarah Bernhardt and a much admired
Countess. Fresh hot-house flowers filled
two delicate Venetian glass vases on the
table, long-leaved green plants stood in the
windows. I began to suspect that the
feminine influence in Fabian Scott's life was

strong enough already, and I felt that any idea of an appeal to a bachelor's sense of loneliness must straightway be given up. There was another point, however, on which I felt more sanguine. Fabian had no private means, his tastes were evidently expensive, and he had had no engagement since the summer. Having made up my mind that to marry my little Babiole to this man was the only thing that would restore her to health and hope (about happiness I could but be doubtful), I could not afford to shrink from the means.

I had been listening with one ear to Fabian, who never wanted much encouragement to talk. He treated me to a long monologue on the low ebb to which art of all kinds had sunk in England, to the prevailing taste for burlesque in literature, and on the stage, and for 'Little Toddlekins' on the walls of picture galleries.

'I thought burlesque had gone out,' I suggested.

He turned upon me fiercely, having finished his breakfast, and being occupied in striding up and down the room.

'Not at all,' he said emphatically. 'What is farcical comedy but burlesque of the most vicious kind? Burlesque of domestic life, throwing ridicule on virtuous wives and jealous husbands, making heroes and heroines of men and women of loose morals? What is melodrama but burlesque of incidents and of passions, fatiguing to the eye and stupefying to the intellect? I repeat, art in England is a dishonoured corpse, and the man who dares to call himself an artist, and to talk about his art with any more reverence than a grocer feels for his sanded sugar, or a violin-seller for his sham Cremonas, is treated with the derision one would show to a modern Englishman who should fall down and worship a mummy.'

All which, being interpreted, meant that Mr. Fabian Scott saw no immediate prospect of an engagement good enough for his deserts.

'Well, even if art is in a bad way, artists still seem to rub on very comfortably,' I said, glancing round the room.

Fabian swept the place with a contemptuous glance from right to left, as if it had been an ill-kept stable.

'One finds a corner to lay one's head in, of course,' he admitted disdainfully; 'but even that may be gone to-morrow,' he added darkly, plunging one hand into a suggestive heap of letters and papers on a side table as he passed it.

'Bills?' I asked cheerfully.

He gave me a tragic nod and strode on.

'You should marry,' I ventured boldly,

'some girl with seven or eight hundred a year, for instance, with a little love of art on her own account to support yours.'

Fabian stopped in front of me with his arms folded. He was the most unstagey actor on the stage, and the stagiest off I ever met. He gave a short laugh, tossing back his head.

'A girl with seven hundred a year marry *me*, an *artist!* My dear fellow, you have been in Sleepy Hollow too long. You form your opinions of life on the dark ages.'

'No I don't,' I said very quietly. 'I know a girl with eight hundred a year, who likes you well enough to marry you if you were to ask her.'

'These rapid modern railway journeys— A heavy breakfast—with perhaps a glass of cognac on an empty stomach'—murmured Fabian softly, gazing at me with kindly compassion.

'She is seventeen, the daughter of an artist, an artist herself by every instinct. Her name is Babiole Ellmer,' I went on composedly.

Fabian started.

'Babiole Ellmer! Pretty little Babiole!' he cried, with affectionate interest at once apparent in his manner; 'but,' he hesitated and flushed slightly, 'I don't understand. The little girl—dear little thing she was, I remember her quite well, with her coquettish Scotch cap and her everlasting blushes. She was no heiress then, certainly.'

A bitter little thought of the different manner in which he would have treated her in that case crossed my mind. 'I've adopted her. I allow her eight hundred a year during my life, and of course afterwards——'

I nodded; he nodded. It was all understood. Fabian had grown suddenly quiet and thoughtful, and I knew that Babiole had

gained her precious admirer's heart. He
liked her, that was my comfort, my excuse.
His face had lighted up at the remembrance
of her; and as she would bring with her
an income large enough to prevent his being
even burdened with her maintenance, I felt
that I was heaping upon his head too much
joy for a mortal to deserve, and that he
accepted it more calmly than was meet. It
is a curious experience to have to be thankful to see another person receive, almost
with indifference, a prize for which one
would gladly have given twenty years of life.

'She is a most beautiful and charming
girl,' he said, after a pause, in a new tone of
respect. Eight hundred a year and 'expecta-
tions' put such a splendid mantle of dignity
on the shoulders of a little wild damsel in
a serge frock. 'Do you know, I thought,
Harry, you would end by marrying her
yourself!'

I only laughed and said, oh no, I was a confirmed bachelor. But it was in my mind to tell him how much obliged I felt for his contribution towards my domestic felicity.

I presently said that I had some business to transact, that I had to pay a visit to my lawyer. This young man's complacent beatitude since he had discovered a not unpleasant way out of his difficulties was beginning to jar upon me furiously. So we made an appointment for the evening, and I took myself off.

When I made my excuse to Fabian I really had some idea in my mind of calling upon a solicitor and having a deed drawn up, settling £800 a year on Babiole. But I reflected, as soon as I was alone, that I should make a better guardian than the law, and that I should do as well to keep control over her allowance. I would alter my will on her wedding-day, just as I must have done if it had been my own. A trace of cowardice strengthened this resolution, for I look upon a visit to a lawyer much as I do upon a visit to a dentist, with this difference, that the latter really does sometimes relieve you of your pain, while the former relieves you of nothing but your money.

So I found myself wandering about my old haunts, glancing up at the windows of clubs of which I had once been a member, and feeling a strong desire to enter their doors once more, and see what change eight years had brought about in my old acquaintances. I had long ago lost all acute sensitiveness about my own altered appearance; there was so very little in common between the 'Handsome Harry' of twenty-four and the scarred gray-haired backwoodsman of thirty-two, that I looked upon them as two distinct persons, and I remained for a few moments confounded by my exceeding

astonishment, when a familiar voice cried,
'Hallo, Maude!' and I found my hand in
the grasp of an important-looking gentleman,
who, as a slim lad, had been one of my
constant companions. He now represented
a small Midland town in Parliament, in the
Conservative interest, seemed amazed that
I had not heard of his speech in favour of
increasing the incomes of bishops, and
confided to me his hopes of getting an
appointment in the Foreign Office when 'his
party' came into power again. I said I
hoped he would, but I inwardly desired that
it might not be a post of great responsibility,
for I found my friend addle-patted to an
extent I had never dreamed of in the old
days, when we backed the same horses and
loved the same ladies. He insisted on taking me into the Carlton, where I met some
more of the old set, who all seemed glad to
see me, but with whom I now felt curiously

out of sympathy. It was not so much that
my politics had veered round, as that, living
an independent and isolated life, I was not
bound to hold fast to traditions and prejudices, like these men who were in the
thick of the fight. I had gone into the club
seeking distraction from my thoughts, trying
to reawaken my old sympathies. I went out
again after an hour of animated and friendly
talk with my acquaintances of eight years
ago, more solitary, more isolated than ever.
Yet when they had tried to persuade me
to come back to life again, being all of
opinion that existence by one's self in the
Highlands was tantamount to a state of
suspended animation, I had answered it was
not unlikely that I might do so.

For the game must be carried on still
when Babiole was married; but not with the
old rules.

I had another interview with Fabian

that evening, for we dined at the Criterion together. It was arranged that he should spend Christmas at Larkhall with me, and it was tacitly understood that he would use this opportunity of assuring Miss Ellmer that her image had never been absent from his mind, and that he could have no rest until she had promised to become his wife at an early date.

I left King's Cross by the nine o'clock train that night, having decided on this course suddenly, when I found I was in too restless a mood to be able to get either sleep or entertainment in London. Arriving at Aberdeen at 2.15 on the following afternoon, I caught the three o'clock train to Ballater, and got to Larkhall before six. It was quite dark by that time, and the lamp was shining through the blind of the sitting-room window at the cottage. I knocked at the door, which was opened by Babiole; she held a candle in her left hand, and by its light I saw her

eyes and cheeks were burning with excitement.

'I knew your knock,' she said tremulously,
as she gave me a hot dry hand, 'though I
did not expect you so soon.'

Here Mrs. Ellmer rushed out of the
sitting-room, fell upon me, and insisted upon
my sitting down to tea with them.

'And how have you been since I left?' I
said to the girl.

'Don't ask, Mr. Maude,' interrupted
her mother. 'I'm sure you would have felt
flattered if you could have seen her. She's
been just like a wild bird in a cage, never
still for two minutes, and half the time with
her face glued to the window, cold as it is;
as if that would make you come back any
faster.'

Babiole hung her head; she may have
blushed, poor child, but her cheeks had been
so hot and burning ever since my entrance,

that no deepening of their colour could be noticed.   I concluded that she had given no hint to her mother of her surmises concerning the object of my journey.

'Well,' said I, 'leading such solitary lives as we do up here, of course the absence of one person makes a great difference.   In fact, my own solitude has begun to prey upon me so much, that—that I rushed up to London on purpose to try to find a friend to spend Christmas up here, and make things livelier for us all.'

'Well,' said Mrs. Ellmer, 'that is an idea, to be sure.   I confess I have been eaten up with wonder at your suddenly going off like that, and have been guessing myself quite silly as to the reason of it.'

'And did Babiole guess too?' I asked lightly, looking at the girl, who sat very quietly, with her eyes fixed upon my face.

'Oh no, she has given up all such childish

amusements as that,' said Mrs. Ellmer rather
sadly. 'There would never be so much as a
laugh to be heard in the place now if I didn't
keep up my spirits.'

'Well, she must open her mouth now, at
any rate. Now, Babiole, can you guess
who it is who is coming to spend Christmas
with us?'

In an instant the strained expression left
her face, a great light flashed into her eyes,
and seemed to irradiate every feature.

'I think you have guessed,' said I gently.

She got up quickly and opened the side-
board, as if looking for something; but I
think, from the attitude of her bent head,
and from the solemn peace that was on her
face when she returned to us, that she had
followed her first impulse to breathe a silent
thanksgiving to God.

'Will you have some quince-marmalade,
Mr. Maude?' she asked, as she came back

to the table with a little glass dish in her hand.

And she leaned over my shoulder to help me to the preserve, while her mother, who had guessed with great glee the name of my Christmas visitor, was still overflowing with exultation at the great news. For she did not once doubt the object of his coming, which, indeed, I had suggested by a delicate archness in which I took some pride.

Shortly after tea I rose to go, being tired out with my two rapid and sleepless journeys. Mrs. Ellmer bade me good-night with kind concern for my fatigue.

'Indeed, I don't think travelling agrees with you, or else you tried to do too much in your short visit, for you look drawn, and worn, and ill, and ten years older than when you started,' she said solicitously.

'Yes, I'm getting too old for dissipation,' I said lightly.

Babiole was standing by the door; she was watching me affectionately, and had evidently some private and particular communication to make to me, by the impatience with which she rattled the door-handle. At last I had shaken hands with Mrs. Ellmer and had got out into the passage. The girl shut the room door quickly and threw herself upon my arm, giving at last free rein to her excitement and passionate gratitude. The gaze of her pure eyes, shining, not with earthly passion, but with the ecstatic light of a dying saint, who sees the heavens opening to receive him, struck a new fear into my heart. The happiness this child-woman looked for was something which Fabian Scott, artist though he was, with splendid verbal aspirations and chivalrous devotions, would not even understand. As she poured forth soft whispering thanks for my goodness—she knew it was all my doing, she said; she had even guessed beforehand what I was going to do—I felt my eyes grow moist and my voice husky.

'My child,' I whispered back, 'don't thank me. It hurts me, for I am not sure that I am not bringing upon you a great and terrible misfortune.'

'Don't be afraid,' she said, shaking her head with that far-off look in her eyes which told so plainly that she saw into a life which could not be lived on earth; 'you think I am romantic, fanciful; that I expect more from this man than his love can ever give me. Oh, but you don't know,' and she looked straight up into my face, with that piercing dreamy earnestness that made her see, not the yearning tenderness of the eyes into which she looked, but only the kind guardian's mind to be convinced. 'You don't know how well I understand. He would never have thought of me again if you had not gone to him and said—I don't know what, but just the thing you knew would touch him, with pity or with pride that a poor little girl could love him so.'   I almost shivered at the dreary distance which lay between this surmise and the truth.   'But I don't mind ; I know that I love him so much, that when he knows and feels what I would do for him, it will make him happy.   You know,' she went on more earnestly still, 'it isn't for him to love me that I have been craving and praying all this time, it was for a sight of his face, or for a letter that he had written himself with his own hand.'

She took my sympathy with her for granted now, and poured this confession out to me quite simply, feeling sure that I understood, as indeed I did to my cost.   But after this I thought it wise to try to calm down this exultation of feeling, by certain grandmotherly platitudes about the difficulties of

married life, the disillusions one had to suffer,
the forbearance one had to show, to all of
which she listened very submissively and
well, but with an evident conviction that she
knew quite as much about the matter as I did.
Then I bade her good-night, and she stood
in the porch, wrapt up in her plaid, until I had
reached my own door, for I heard her clear
young voice sing out a last 'good-night' as I
went in.

Poor little girl! She could not know how
her gratitude cut me to the heart.

CHAPTER XVIII

THE ten days before Christmas we spent on the whole happily. Mrs. Ellmer burst into tears on my informing her of the allowance I proposed to make to her daughter, and sobbed out hysterically, 'My own child to be able to keep a carriage! Oh! if poor mamma could have known!'

This announcement, when made to Babiole by her mother, was the one drawback to her happiness. She implored me to change my mind, little guessing, poor child, what other change that would have involved. I was very angry with Mrs. Ellmer for spoiling the girl's perfect bliss by this vulgar detail, which it had been necessary to impart to the mother, but which I had particularly desired to with-hold for the present from the daughter's more sensitive ears. I had hard work to comfort her, but I succeeded at last by reminding her that she was under my guardianship, and that it was my pride to see my ward cut a handsome figure in the world.

I almost think, if it does not sound far-fetched to say so, that the girl enjoyed those ten days with me, prattling about her lover and endowing him with gifts of beauty and nobility and wisdom which neither he nor any man I ever met possessed, more than the fortnight of feverish joy in his actual presence which followed. Not that Fabian was disappointing as a *fiancé;* far from it. He had the gift of falling into raptures easily, and he fell in love with his destined bride as promptly as heart could desire. But the imaginative quality, which formed so important a feature of the young girl's romantic passion, caused her at first to shrink from his vehement caresses as at a blow to her ideal, while on the other hand the light touch of his fingers would send a convulsive shiver through her whole frame.

How did I know all this? . I can scarcely tell. And yet it is true, and I learnt it early in Fabian's short visit. As the savage knows the signs of the sky, so did I, living by myself, study to some purpose the gentle nature whose smiles made my happiness.

When Fabian left us at the end of a fortnight, it was settled that the wedding was to take place in six weeks' time at Newcastle. I had a prejudice against my ward's being married in Scotland, where I conceived, rightly or wrongly, that a certain looseness of the marriage-tie prevailed. On the other hand, I would not let her go to London to be married, being of opinion that

such a bride was worth a journey. So Mrs.
Ellmer having some relations at Newcastle,
she and her daughter spent there the three
weeks immediately preceding the ceremony.
I missed them dreadfully during those three
weeks, and was not without a vague hope
somewhere down in the depths of my heart
that something unforeseen might happen to
prevent the marriage. But when I arrived
at Newcastle on the evening before the
appointed day, Fabian was already there,
everybody was in the highest spirits ; and
Mrs. Ellmer's Newcastle cousins, rather
proud of the position in 'society' which
they were assured the bride was going to
hold, had undertaken to provide a handsome
wedding breakfast.

I gave her away next morning, in the old
church with its crowned tower which they
now call a cathedral. I think perhaps she
guessed something more than I would have

had her know in the vestry when the service was over, when I asked her for a kiss and fell a-trembling as she granted it ; at any rate she turned very white and grave in the midst of her happiness, and thenceforth dropped her voice to a humble half-whisper whenever she spoke to me. She had been married in her travelling dress, an innovation rather alarming to Newcastle ; but she looked so pretty in her first silk gown—a dark brown—and in the long sealskin mantle that had been my wed- ding present, that I think some of the damsels at the breakfast decided that this fashion was one to be followed.

The bride and bridegroom left us early, more, I think, because Fabian found both breakfast and speeches heavy than because there was any need to hurry for the train. I having no such excuse, and being treated as a great personage with a Monte-Christo-like habit of dowering marriageable maidens, was

forced to remain. I made a speech, I forget
what about, which was received with laughter
and enthusiasm. The only things I remember
about the people were the strong impression
of dull and commonplace provincialism which
their speech and manner made upon me, and
that on the other hand, a little quiet maiden
of seventeen or so, who wore a very rusty
frock and was awkwardly shy, astonished me
by quoting Tacitus in the original, and
proved to be quite an appallingly learned
person.

When I could get away I bade farewell to
Mrs. Ellmer, who touched my heart by crying
over my departure. She had made arrangements to stay in Newcastle with an aunt who
was getting old, and who felt inclined for the
cheap charity of discharging her servant and
taking the active and industrious little woman
to live with her. Mrs. Ellmer was to take
care of Ta-ta till my return. Outside the

door Ferguson met me with my old portmanteau ready on a cab.   In five minutes I
was off on my travels again.

I was out of England altogether for four
years, during which, among other little expeditions, I traversed America from the southern-
most point of Terra del Fuego to the land of
the Eskimos. I heard nothing of Babiole or her
husband, nor did I make any efforts to hear
anything about them, being of opinion that a
man and his wife settle down to life together
best without any of that outside interference
which it is so difficult for those who love them
to withhold, when they see things going amiss
with the young household. At the end of
four years, I had said to myself, they will
have obtained a rudimentary knowledge of
each other's character. Babiole will be a
woman and will no longer see the reflex of
the divinity in any man ; the experiment of
marriage will be in working order, and one

will be able to judge the results.   I had not
forgotten them, indeed I had thought of them
continually.   I had taken care that Babiole's
allowance was regularly paid; but my second
sentimental disappointment having found me
some sort of a misanthrope, had cured me of
my misanthropy; and a freer intercourse with
men and women, and a particular study of
such married couples as I met convinced me
that the mutual attraction of man and woman
towards each other is so great that merely
negative qualities in the one sex count as
virtues in the eyes of the other, and that a
husband and wife who will only abstain from
being actively disagreeable to one another
are in a fair way towards attaining a gentle
mutual enthusiasm which will make the
grayest of human lives seem fair.   Now
Babiole could never be actively disagreeable
to anybody; and surely not even a disappointed artist, and no artist is so disappointed

as he who is all but the most successful, could
be actively disagreeable to Babiole.

But my philosophy had weak points, which
I was soon abruptly to discover.

It was in the month of March that I came
back to England and put up at the Bedford
Hotel, Covent Garden.   Fabian and his wife
lived in a flat at Bayswater, the address of
which I had taken care to obtain.   Although
I was much excited at the thought of seeing
them, I was by no means anxious to antici-
pate the meeting, which I had decided should
not take place until tailor and hatter and
hair-dresser had done their best to remove all
traces of barbarism.   My beard I had decided
to retain, but it must be now the beard of
Bond Street, and not that of the prairies.   In
the meantime I took a solitary stall at the
theatre where Fabian was playing, with some
vague idea of gaining a premonitory insight
into the course of his matrimonial career.

A keen sensation of something which I
regret to say was not wholly disappointment
shot through me as I perceived that, so far
from having acquired any touch of the comfortable and commonplace which is the out-
ward and visible sign of an inward domestic
tranquillity, Fabian was leaner, more haggard
than ever. He had grown more petulant
and irritable, too, as I gathered from his
annoyance with a large and lively party of
very well dressed people who sat in one of
the boxes nearest the stage, and who, without
transgressing such lax bonds of good breeding
as usually control the occupants of stalls and
boxes, evidently found more entertainment in
each other than in the people on the stage.

I glanced up at the box, following instinctively the direction of Fabian's eyes, and
saw an ugly but clever-looking young man
very much occupied with a pale sad-faced
lady ; two very young men and two other

ladies, both with the dead-white complexions
and black dresses which have been of late so
popular with the half world and its imitators,
formed the rest of the occupants.

Before the end of the first scene in which
he was engaged, Fabian had recognised me,
and in the pause between the acts a note from
him was brought to me by one of the atten-
dants asking me to 'go and speak to Babiole,
and to come home to supper with them.'

Speak to Babiole! Why, then, she must
be in the theatre! I got up and peered about
with my glasses ; but though I could see well
into every part of the house, I could discover
no one in the least like my little witch of the
hills. After a careful inspection, I decided
that she must be one of three or four ladies
who were hidden by the curtains of the boxes
in which they sat. In this belief I had resumed my seat and given up the search when,
just as the curtain was rising upon the next

act, and I glanced up again at the people
who had excited Fabian's wrath, a look, a
movement of the pale sad-looking lady suddenly attracted my attention. I raised my
glasses again in consternation; for, changed
as she was, with all her pretty colour faded,
the bright light gone from her eyes, the soft
outlines of her little face altered and sharpened,
there was now no possibility of mistaking the
melancholy and listless lady who was still
absorbing the attention of the clever-looking
man beside her for any other than my old
pupil.

Through the remaining two acts of the
piece I scarcely dared to look at her; everything seemed to indicate the total failure of
the match I had made. I wanted to escape
for that night any further indictment than my
fears brought against me, but I was scarcely
outside the theatre after the performance
when a hand was laid upon my shoulder in

the crowd, and Fabian, who had hurried round to meet me, led me back into the building and presented me to his wife. The young fellow who had been so devoted in the box was with her still, together with one of the ladies in black. Fabian's manner to me was as emphatically cordial as ever, and showed no trace of a grievance against me; but Babiole's was utterly changed. She was talking to her companion when she first caught sight of me, as I passed through the swinging doors with her husband, and made my way toward her among footmen and plush-enveloped ladies. The words she was uttering suddenly froze on her lips, and the last vestige of colour left her pale face as if at some sight at least as horrible as unexpected. Before I reached her she had recovered herself, however, and was holding out her hand, not indeed with the old frank pleasure, but with a very gracious conventional welcome.

'Fancy, my dear,' said Fabian, 'the villain
has been in the country two whole days without thinking of calling upon us. These
sneaking ways must be punished upon the
spot, and I pronounce therefore that he be
immediately seized and carried off to supper.'

I protested that I was too tired to do anything but fall asleep.

'Well, you can fall asleep at our place
just as well as at yours. And that reminds
me that you had better sleep there. We've
plenty of room, and we can send the boy for
your things.'

'Thanks. Its awfully kind of you, Scott,
but I couldn't do that, I have an appointment
at——'

'There that second excuse spoils it all. A
first excuse may awaken only incredulity, a
second inevitably rouses contempt. You shall
sleep where you like, but you must sup with
us.'

'You will bring Mr. Maude with you in a hansom, then, Fabian,' said his wife, who had not joined in the discussion, 'for Mrs. Capel is coming with me.'

Fabian, who had been only coldly civil to Mrs. Capel, the lady in black, looked annoyed, but had to acquiesce in these arrangements. We saw the ladies into the brougham, Fabian gave a curt good-night to the clever-looking young man, and then we jumped into a hansom and drove towards Bayswater.

I confess I wished myself at the other end of the world, especially as I began to think that, while my hostess certainly was not anxious for my society, my host was chiefly actuated in his obstinate hospitality by the desire to show that he bore me no malice. Thus when he congratulated me on being still a bachelor it was in such a magnanimous tone that I found myself forced to express a hope that he did not envy me my freedom.

'I must not say that I do,' said he, with more magnanimity than ever. 'Still it is but frank to own that personal experience of marriage has confirmed my previous convictions instead of reversing them.   In short, to put it plainly, I found soon after my marriage, as all men in my position must sooner or later find, that I had to choose between being my wife's ideal of a good husband or my own ideal of a good artist.   I found that a good woman is twice as exacting as a divine Art; for while Art only demands the full and free exercise of your working faculties in her service, a woman insists on the undivided empire of your very thoughts; she must have a full, true, and particular account of your dreams; you must not run, jump, sneeze, or cough but in her honour.'

'And you chose the Art, I suppose,' I said, trying not to speak coldly.

'My dear boy, I really had no choice.

Babiole and I each wanted a slave ; but while I demanded a fellow-slave in the labours of my life, this pretty little lady only wished for a human footstool for her pretty little feet.'

'But I cannot understand. Babiole was always as submissive as a lamb, a dog, anything you like that is gentle and docile.'

'My dear Maude, at the time you speak of she was unwedded. Now just as the horse, in himself a noble animal, corrupts and depraves every man with whom he comes in contact, from the groom to the jockey, so does intercourse with man, the king of creatures, speedily destroy in woman all the traces of those good qualities with which, in deference to the poets, we will concede her to have been originally endowed.'

'I know nothing about that,' said I bluntly, 'but if Babiole Ellmer has been anything short of a perfectly true-hearted

wife, I will stake my solemn oath that she
has been harnessed to a damned bad husband.'

I was cold and wet with overmastering
indignation, or I should not have blurted
out my opinion so coarsely. Fabian was
on fire directly, gesticulating with his hands,
glaring with his eyes, in his old impulsive
style.

' Do you mean to accuse me of telling you
lies ? Do you mean to insinuate that I have
not treated your ward as a gentleman should
treat his wife, especially when she is the
adopted daughter of his best friend ? Do
you think I should dare to look you in
the face if I had failed in my duty towards
her ?'

' If you were one of the " common rabble
of humanity " you despise so much, I should
tell you you had failed in your duty very
much. As you belong to a clique which

considers itself above such rules, I tell you
frankly that Art wouldn't suffer a jot if you
did neglect her, while this poor child does;
and that if you were to act like Garrick,
write like Shakespeare, and paint like
Raphael, it wouldn't excuse you for the
change between your wife on her wedding
day and your wife to-night.'

'You are very severe,' said Fabian, who
was shaking with excitement and passion.
' If you are really so lost to a man's common
sense as to take it for granted already that
the fault is all on one side, you must pardon
me if I set your remarks down to the ravings
of infatuation.'

There was a pause. This thrust told, for
indeed a great wave of bitter and passionate
regret at the loss beyond recall of my pretty
witch of the hills was drowning my calmer
reason and making me rude and savage
beyond endurance. We had just self-control

enough left to remain silent for the remaining
few minutes of the drive, both quaking with
rage, and both ashamed, I of my explosion,
he, I hope, of the lameness of his explana-
tions. The hansom stopped at the mansions,
on the third floor of one of which Mr. and
Mrs. Scott lived. I jumped out first, raised
my hat, and excusing myself coldly and
formally, was hurrying away, when Fabian,
regardless of the cabman, who thought it was
a dodge, and hallooed after him, followed me
at a run, put his arm through mine, and
dragged me back again.

'Can't quarrel with you, Harry,' he said
affectionately, 'Say it's all my fault if you
like, but hear both sides first. Come in,
come in I tell you.'

And having given vent to his feelings in
a volley of eloquent abuse to the shouting
cabman, he tossed him his fare and led me
into the house.

Curiously enough, the emotion which seemed to choke me as I mounted the stairs and stood outside the door of Babiole's home, disappeared entirely as soon as the door was opened to admit us. For there, standing in the little entrance hall, at the open door of the drawing-room, was the slim pale lady with pleasant conventional manners, and the pretty little meaningless laugh of a desire to please. We followed her into the room, which was charmingly furnished, lighted by coloured lights, scented by foreign perfumes, and hung with drawings and engravings of which the mistress of the house was very proud. She was so lively and bright, criticised the piece in which her husband was playing so unmercifully, and said so many witty and amusing things during supper, that I forgot Babiole in Mrs. Scott, and was only recalled to a remembrance of her identity by an occasional gesture or a tone of the voice.

If I had not seen her in the theatre first I might have thought she was a happy wife, as, if I had not remembered the round rosy cheeks and sparkling eyes of the little maid of Craigendarroch, I might have admired the piquant delicacy of the small white face before me, in which the gray eyes looked abnormally large and dark.

After enjoying myself greatly, though not quite unreservedly, I had risen to take leave, when Fabian, suddenly remembering that he had some proofs to send off which were already overdue at a publisher's, asked me if I would mind waiting while he finished correcting them. It wouldn't take a minute. He had his hand upon the door which led from the dining-room to the little den he called his study, when his wife, in almost terror-struck entreaty, rushed towards him and begged him to leave it till next day.

'I can't, Bab; they must go by the first

post, and you know very well I shan't be up
in time to do them.'

'I'll do them for you,' she said eagerly.

'No, no, don't tease,' said her husband
authoritatively, 'take Mr. Maude into the
drawing-room and play him something,' and
he pushed her off and left the room.

She turned to me with a smiling shrug of
the shoulders, and said playfully, 'See what
it is to be a down-trodden wife.'   Then,
leading the way into the drawing-room, and
seating herself at once at the piano, she
dashed into a lively waltz air.   But it suddenly occurred to me that she was possessed
with some strange fear of being alone with
me, and this idea broke the spell of her
brilliant manner, and reduced me to shy and
stupid silence.

CHAPTER XIX

I HAD sat down in a low chair near the piano, and I remained looking at a rug under my feet as my hostess went on playing one bright piece after another with scarcely a pause between.

'I know very well,' she said at last, 'that you don't care for any of this music a bit. Men call it rubbish, and affect to despise it, just as they do high-heeled boots, dainty millinery, and lots of other pretty frivolous things.'

'I don't despise it, I assure you. It is very inspiriting, at least—it would chime in well with one's feelings if one were in high spirits.'

'Still I know you are ascribing my change
of taste in music to a great moral deteriora-
tion. But listen——'

She broke off in a gavotte she was playing,
and sang 'Auld Robin Gray' so that every
note seemed to strike on my heart. In the
old time among the hills Babiole used to sing
it to me, in a wild, sweet, bird-like voice that
thrilled and charmed me, and made me call
her my little tame nightingale; but the
song I heard now was not the same; there
was a new ring in the pathos, a plaintive
cry that seemed to reach my very soul; and
I listened holding my breath.

When the last note was touched on the
piano, I raised my head with an effort and
looked at her; almost expecting, I believe, to
see tears in her eyes. She was looking at
me, curiously, with a very still face of grave
inquiry. As she met my gaze she looked
down at the keys, and began another waltz.

'Don't play any more,' I said abruptly.

She stopped, and seeming for a moment
rather embarrassed, began to turn over the
leaves of a pile of music on a chair beside her.

'You have learnt to sing, I suppose,' I said
quietly.   'You know I am a Goth in musical
matters, but I can tell that.'

'And of course you are going to tell me
that my fresh untutored voice gave sweeter
music than any singing-master could produce,'
said she, with almost spasmodic liveliness.

'Indeed I am not.   Your singing to-night
not only struck me as being infinitely better
than it used to be from a musician's point of
view, but it expressed the sentiment of the
song with a vividness that caused me acute
pain.'

I had risen from my seat, and was stand-
'ing by the piano.   She shot up at me one of
her old looks, a child's shy appeal for indulgence.

'You have learnt a great deal since I saw
you last; you have become the accomplished
fascinating woman it was your ambition to
be.   I have never met any one more
amusing.'

'Yes,' she said slowly; 'I have fulfilled
my ambition, I suppose.'   For a few minutes
she remained busy with the leaves of the
music, while I still watched her, and noticed
how the plump healthy red hands of the
mountain girl had dwindled into the slender
white ones of the London lady.   Then she
leaned forward over the keyboard, and
asked curiously, 'Which do you like best,
the little wild girl whom you used to teach,
or the accomplished woman who amuses
you?'

'I like them both, in quite a different
way.'   If I am not mistaken her face fell.
'To tell you the truth, I now find it hard
to connect the two.   I love the memory of

the little wild girl who used to sit by my side, and make me think myself a very wise person by the eagerness with which she listened to me, while I laid down the law on all matters human and divine; and I have a profound admiration for the gracious lady whom I meet to-night for the first time.'

'Admiration!' She repeated the word in a low voice, rather scornfully, touching the keys of the piano lightly, and looking at me with a dreary smile. Then she turned her head away, but not quickly enough to hide from me that her eyes were filling with tears.

A great thrill of pity and tenderness for the forlorn soul thus suddenly revealed drew me nearer to her, and I said, leaning towards the little bending figure—

'I did not mean to pain you, Babiole. You cannot think that, caring for you as I used to do as if you had been my own child, I have lost all feeling for you now.'

She turned quickly towards me again, biting her under lip as she fixed her eyes wistfully, eagerly, upon my face. Then with tears rolling down her cheeks, she laid her head on my arm, and clinging to my hand, to my sleeve, began to sob and to whisper incoherent words of gladness at my coming.

'My child, my child!' I said hoarsely, with a passionate yearning to comfort the fragile little creature whose whole body was trembling with repressed sobs. I got into a sort of frenzy as she went on helplessly crying, and eloquence soon ran dry in my efforts to comfort her. 'Look here, child, this won't do any good. Hold up your head, Babiole; for goodness sake don't go on like this, my dear, or I shall be snivelling myself in a moment,' I said, with more of the same matter-of-fact kind, until she presently looked up and laughed at me through her tears.

'There now, you've quite spoilt yourself

by this nonsense,' I continued severely. 'Go
and put yourself to rights before your husband
comes in.'

And I led her to the looking-glass with
my arm round her, feeling, though I did not
recognise the fact at the time, a great relief
in this little demonstration of an affection
which was growing every moment stronger.

'Do you know,' she asked presently, as
she turned her head away from the glass
before which she had, by some dexterous
feminine sleight of hand with two or three
hairpins, arranged her disordered hair, 'why
Fabian had proofs to correct to-night?'

I confessed with shame that my male
mind had been content with the reason he
had given.

'He wanted to leave me alone with you,'
she explained, 'because he knows what a
strong influence you have over me, and he
hoped that you would give me a lecture.'

'A lecture! What did he want me to lecture on ?'

'Oh, on my general conduct, I suppose; on my acquaintance, intimacy with people he dislikes; on my taking part in amateur theatricals; on a lot of things—on everything in fact.'

'But if your husband can't induce you to do what he wishes, what chance have I, an outsider ?'

'Oh, Mr. Maude, dear Mr. Maude, have you been so long among the hills as to think like that ? Or is it that life was a different thing when you took an active part in it ? It's only in books that husbands are husbands, and wives are wives.'

She had sat down on the sofa beside me, but I was not going to be talked over like that. Her words had roused in me the instinctive antagonism of the sexes, and I got up and walked up and down, an occupation which demanded some care amidst the miniature inlaid furniture with which the small room was somewhat overcrowded.

'You know, my dear,' I began rather drily, looking at the ceiling, which was not far above my head, 'when things get so radically wrong between husband and wife, as they seem to be between you and Fabian, the fault is very seldom all on one side.'

'But it is in this case.'

'Are you sure?'

'Yes, quite sure.'

'You think you are not to blame in the least?'

'In this, no.'

'And that all the fault lies on poor Fabian's side?'

'Oh no.'

'Well, on whose side does it lie then?'

'On yours.'

I stopped short in front of her, and looked

down on the little Dresden china figure, sitting with clasped hands and crossed feet in exasperating demureness on the sofa below me.

'Do you know that you are a confoundedly ungrateful little puss?'

'No, I'm not,' she answered passionately, raising her head and meeting my gaze with eyes full of fire. 'I think of you by day and by night. I read over the books I read with you, to try to feel as if you were still by my side explaining them to me. I talk to you when I am by myself, I sing my best songs to you, I almost pray to you. But just as the heathen beat their gods and throw them in the dust when they lose a battle, so I, when things go wrong with me, find a consolation in accusing you of being the cause.' She laughed a little as she finished, as if ashamed of her temerity, and anxious to let it pass as a joke. But I held my ground and looked at her steadily.

'That is very flattering,' said I, more moved than I cared to show, 'but it is nothing in support of your accusation. Women, the very best of you, think nothing of bringing against your friends charges which a man——'

She interrupted hastily, 'I brought no charge.'

'You only accused me of deliberately spoiling the lives of two of my dearest friends.'

'No, no, not that; I only said that you brought about our marriage.'

'Which then seemed to you the climax of earthly happiness. Remember, you married him with your eyes open, content not even to expect him to be a good husband. You admitted that yourself. Is it my fault that your love has proved a weaker thing than you thought?'

'Weaker!' This was apparently a new idea to her. She now spoke in a humbler

tone. 'How could I know,' she asked
meekly, 'what strong things it would have
to conquer? I thought all men were something like you—at heart, and that to please
them one had only to try. Oh, and I did
try so hard!'

The poor little face was drawn into piteous lines and wrinkles as she sighed forth
this lament.

'But what has he done, child?'

She shook her head. 'Nothing. If I
could have seen before marriage a diary of
my married life as it would be, I should
have thought, as I did, that I was going into
an earthly paradise. There is nothing wrong
but the atmosphere, and there is only one
thing wanting in that.'

'He does not care for you?' I scarcely
did more than form the words with my lips,
but the answering tears rolled down her
cheeks again at once.

'Not a bit.   At least, not so much as *you* care for To-to or—Janet.   And it isn't his fault.   He is perfectly kind to me in his fashion, admires the way I have worked to please him, is grieved that I am dissatisfied with the result.   Only—he did not take me in —of his own accord, and so I have remained always—outside.   That's all !'

She spread out her little hands, and clasped them again, with a plaintive gesture of resignation.

'And—and if I seem ungrateful you must forgive me ; I've never been able to tell it all to any one for all these four years.'

I was stricken with remorse, but I dared not give it the least expression for fear of the lengths to which it might carry me.

I made another journey among the gipsy tables and the pestilent *bric-à-brac*, and returning sat down, not on the sofa beside her, but in a chair a few feet away.   I took

a book up from a table by my side; I remember that it was *Marmion*, and that it had
very exquisite illustrations.

'How about these friends, then, whose
intimacy your husband disapproves of?'

'Oh, those!' contemptuously. 'One
doesn't open one's heart quite wide to such
friends as those.'

'Then if you care about them so little,
why not give them up and please your
husband?'

'One must be intimate with somebody,'
she said entreatingly, 'even if it's only a
tea-drinking and scandal-talking intimacy.'

'But why with these particular people?'

'Because we all have a particular grievance: we all have bad husbands. At least
—no, Fabian's not a bad husband,' she corrected hastily; 'but we are all dissatisfied
with our husbands.'

'Perhaps the husbands of those ladies I

saw with you at the theatre—forgive me if I
am making a rude and ridiculous mistake—
are dissatisfied with them?' I suggested,
very meekly and mildly.

'I daresay they are,' she answered, flushing. 'The less a man has of domestic
virtues, the more he invariably expects from
his wife.'

'I am not surprised that Fabian shrinks
from the thought of your looking as they do.'

'You mean that they make up their faces?
Mr. Maude, Mr. Maude, listen. A woman
must have something to live upon, to live
for. If through her fault or her misfortune,
there is not love enough at home to keep her
heart warm, she will—I don't say she ought,
but she does—look about for a make-shift,
and finds it in the admiration of some lad
younger than herself, who is ready to give
more than he ever hopes to receive. The
boys like dyed hair and powdered faces,

they think it "chic." But my friends are not the depraved creatures Fabian would like to make out.'

I was horribly shocked at her defence of these ladies, for it showed a bitter knowledge of some of the world's ways that jarred on the lips of a woman of twenty.

'I should not like to see you consoling yourself like that.'

She looked at me frankly, and her face relaxed into a faint smile as she spoke.

'You need not be afraid; now you are back in England, I don't want any other consolation. I can't forget that there is goodness in the world while I can see you and hear from you. You are going to settle in town?' she added quickly and anxiously.

'No, I had not thought of doing so. I am going back to Lark——' Before I could finish the word she was at my feet, kneeling on a cushion and leaning over the arm of my chair with her face distorted by strong excitement.

'No, no, not Larkhall ; you must not go back to Larkhall,' she whispered earnestly 'Promise me you won't go there, promise, promise.'

'Why, what's the matter ?   Where should I go but to the only home I have had for eleven years ?'

'Yes, but it isn't safe now.   If I tell you why you will only laugh at me.'

'No, child, I should be ungrateful to laugh at any proof of your interest in me.'

She put her hand on my arm, earnestly pressing it at every other word to give emphasis to her warning.

'My father—you remember him—he is dissatisfied with my marriage. He says you promised to be answerable for my happiness, and he shall make you answer for breaking faith with him.'

'But I have not——'

'I know. I told him that, I told him everything; that I was dying, like the idiot I was, for the love of a man who didn't care for me. He has taken to drink — much worse than before — and he is impatient, savage, and won't listen to reason. He will do nothing but repeat, again and again, "He said he would answer for it, and he shall."'

'But he doesn't even know I have returned.'

'He said you were sure to fly back to the old nest, and—listen, Mr. Maude, for I know this is true; he has gone up there to lie in wait for you. And remember, a man who has one crazed idea and won't listen to anything but his own mad impulses, is more dangerous than one who is angry with good cause.'

'Poor fellow, I think he has good cause.'

'But, Mr. Maude, you don't know what ridiculous things he says!'

'What things?'

'He says that you ought not to have consulted my caprices, but to have married me yourself straight away!'

She began to laugh as she finished, but I stopped her.

'He is quite right.   So I ought to have done.   Unluckily, there was one thing in the way.'

Babiole, who was still on the cushion at my feet, leaning against the arm of my chair as she used to do in the Highlands, was looking interested and deeply surprised.

'One thing in the way!' she echoed softly, looking into my face with earnest scrutiny. 'What—*before* I fell in love with—Fabian?'

'Yes, long before that.'

She hesitated, and her eyes slowly left my

face, while her brows contracted with a
puzzled expression.

'What was it?' she asked at last, in a
whisper.

'I was in love with you.'

I could see very little of her face, but
a shiver passed over her. For a moment I
wondered, sitting quietly back in my chair,
what she thought.

'Didn't you ever guess anything of it,
child, when we had that odd sort of half-en-
gagement?' I asked, in a most loyal tone of
indifference.

She raised her head and looked at me
modestly and solemnly.

'I should as soon have thought,' she said,
in a low unsteady voice, 'that the Arch-
bishop of Canterbury was—in love with me.'

'Aha!' I said with a ridiculous cackling
laugh. 'Then I shouldn't have had much
chance.'

The next moment I knew better. She rose without another word, as the sounds of an opening and shutting door reached our ears. But as she did so she cast upon me one quick, shy, involuntary side-glance, and I knew that my scruples about my ugly face had been worse than thrown away.

The next moment Fabian came into the room.

CHAPTER XX

I LEFT London for Ballater the very next day; and having sent Ferguson on in advance to prepare the place for me, I found Larkhall just as I had left it four years before, down to a newspaper which had been lying on my study table. But the spirit of home had deserted the place; Ta-ta was still at Newcastle. To-to recognised me indeed, but with more sulky impatience at my absence than pleasure at my return. The cottage was shut up and empty; I got the key from Janet after dinner, and wandered through the unused, damp-smelling little rooms. The furniture had been left, by my orders,

just as it had been during the occupation of
Babiole and her mother. But I found that
instead of recalling the child Babiole, as I
had seen her so often flitting about the
sitting-room, or, in the latter days, leaning
back, languid and listless, with glistening
dreamy eyes, in the rocking-chair by the fire,
it was the pale little London lady with pretty
conventional manners and worn weary face
that I was trying to picture to myself in the
uninhabited rooms. I came out again,
locked the door carefully, and finished my
cigar in the porch. It seemed to me a remarkably odd thing that Babiole's degenera-
tion from the faultless angel she used as a
child to appear, into a mere soured and
sorrowful woman who looked six or seven
years more than her age, had deepened my
interest in her, while my knowledge that she
had been lost to me through nothing but my
own diffidence had changed its character.

To get the better of the unhealthy and
morbid state of mind into which I now found
myself falling, I began to break through my
old habits of retirement, and to avail myself
of such society as Ballater and its neighbourhood afforded. The hot weather had begun
early this year, and the summer residents
were already established before my arrival.
I was a sort of 'great unknown' concerning
whom there were floating about many interesting and romantic stories ; therefore I
found no lack of eager acquaintances as soon
as I cared to make them.   Prominent among
these was a certain Mr. Farington, a Liver-
pool solicitor, who, after having made a
yearly retreat to the Highlands each autumn,
had now retired from business and taken the
lease of a large house at the foot of Craigendarroch. He had been married twice, first
to a lady of dazzling pecuniary charms who
had left him one daughter, and after her death

to a large and handsome lady who gave me
a strong impression of having had doubtful
antecedents. This second wife had a num-
erous family, ranging from five years old to
fifteen, between whom and their half-sister
was fixed the gulf of her mother's fortune.

At a very early stage of our acquaintance
the eldest Miss Farington, who was a good-
looking young woman of three and twenty,
with a strong sense of the importance attached
to an income of fifteen hundred a year, had
honoured me by a marked partiality for
which I, in my new sociability, at first felt
grateful. It was pleasant to find some one
who could pass an opinion, even if it was not
a very original opinion, on a picture, a book,
or a landscape, and Miss Farington could
always do that with great precision. Perhaps,
too, it flattered my vanity to be appealed to
as the one representative of high civilisation
amidst barbarian hordes. But when it be-

came plain even to my modest merit that the
lady proposed to annex me, I grew suddenly
coy; and I then found to my surprise that,
diffident as my disfigurement had made me, I
was still, like the rest of my sex, humble only
to one woman, and mightily fatuous as re-
garded the rest.   But if Miss Farington was
merely what one calls 'a nice girl,' with no
particularly conspicuous qualities of alluring
sweetness or captivating vivacity, she had
one virtue which would not have shamed an
ancient Roman—an indomitable resolution
that would not know defeat.

I am not making an idle boast; I am re-
cording a fact when I say that that girl laid
siege to me with a skill and patience which
filled me alternately with admiration, gratitude, and alarm.   She learned my tastes, she
studied my habits, she mastered my opinions,
until I began to think that if a person who
apparently knew me so well could like me

so much, I must be an infinitely more amiable man than I had ever supposed.   This frame of mind naturally led me to look kindly on the lady who had enabled me to make such a pleasing discovery, and I knew myself to be softening to such an extent that I felt that, unless Mr. Farington should leave Ballater before the summer was over, I should be 'a gone coon' before autumn.   If she held on until the evenings grew cold and long, until the winds began to howl about lonely Lark-hall, and to bring swirling showers of dead leaves to the ground with the hissing sound of a beach of pebbles under the retreating waves of a wintry sea, then I felt that I should give way, that I should see in Miss Farington's prosaic gray eyes pleasant do-mestic pictures, in her erect figure and slop-ing shoulders an attraction which to a lonely man, when the deer-stalking and fishing seasons were over, were quite irresistible.

I had had one plaintive little letter from
Babiole, in which she entreated me, in rather
stiff and stilted language, out of which peeped
a most touching anxiety, to beware of her
father, who, she assured me, was more desperate and dangerous in his intentions to do
me harm than she had even dared to suggest
when face to face with me. I wrote back in
a clumsy letter as stiff as her own, but not so
touching, that she need have no fear, as her
father had settled down quietly at Aberdeen.
I dared not tell her the truth, which I
had found out through Ferguson—that Mr.
Ellmer had indeed come up to the Highlands
with the avowed intention of doing me some
desperate harm ; but that, having availed
himself too freely, through his daughter's
generosity, of his favourite indulgences, he
had had an attack of *delirium tremens*, and
had been placed under restraint in the county
lunatic asylum.

Babiole's letter I carried about with me, and sometimes—for loneliness among the hills would make a sentimental fool of the most robust of us—I fancied that the little sheet of paper, in spite of Miss Farington and the domestic pictures, burnt into my heart.

It was in the middle of August, while the weather was still—everywhere but in the Highlands—insufferably hot, that I received a letter from Fabian which gave me a great shock. His wife had been very ill, he said, and although she had now been declared out of danger, she recovered strength so slowly that it had become imperative to send her away somewhere. Mrs. Ellmer, who was now with her, having suggested her old home in the Highlands, the doctor had agreed warmly, and Fabian therefore begged, as an old friend, that I would lend his wife and her mother the cottage for a short time, adding that he was sure I would look after my little favourite until, in a few days' time, he could rejoin her.

I took this letter up to Craigendarroch, and had first a cigar and then a pipe over it. To refuse Fabian's request was impossible; to lend the cottage and go away myself would be inhospitable and suspicious; to lend it and stay would be dangerous. With the last whiffs of tobacco an inspiration came. I swung back home, wrote back to Fabian that Larkhall itself, the cottage, the garden, the stables, and every toolshed about the place were entirely at Mrs. Scott's disposal, together with all the live stock, human and otherwise; and that she had only to fix the time of her arrival and Mrs. Ellmer's.

The letter finished and put in the bag, I had a glass of sherry; and fortified by that and by an heroic sense of duty, I sallied forth in the direction of the Mill o' Sterrin, in which neighbourhood Miss Farington, who did everything by rule, was always to be found district-visiting on a Thursday.

I suppose no man with ever so little brain or ever so little heart, who has deliberately made up his mind to propose to a girl, sees the moment approaching without a certain trepidation. I own that when I saw the moment and Miss Farington approaching together, although I had very little doubt about her answer, and very little enthusiasm about the result, I had a thumping at my heart and a singing in my ears. With the memory of Babiole and the thought of her visit in my mind, not even the sherry would cast a glamour over those exceedingly sloping shoulders, which seemed almost to argue some moral deficiency, some terrible lack of some quality without which no woman's character is complete. In the meantime, she was bearing down upon me, and I was still without an opening speech. But she was not.

'What a treat to see you in this part of the world, Mr. Maude,' said she, holding out her hand. 'I confess I did you the injustice to think you would forget your promise.'

'Promise!' I repeated vaguely. 'I am afraid I must confess——'

'You had forgotten?' she said smiling. 'Really this is too bad.'

'At least, you see, I hadn't forgotten that this is the way you always walk on a Thursday,' said I, with a look that was intended to convey much.

'And had forgotten my beautiful site for a new school!'

However, she was more pleased with me for what I had remembered than angry for what I had forgotten.

'At any rate you can come and see it now,' she said, and turning back she led the

way towards a broad meadow in the valley
of the Muick, with a fair view of the little
river and of the hills beyond, which would
have been a very good site for a school, if a
school had been needed.

'An awfully nice place for it,' I agreed,
as she expatiated upon the merits of a rising ground with drainage towards the
river, and shelter from the woods above.
'And if the school ever gets built, I
expect there will be only one thing it will
want.'

'Go on, though I know what you are going
to say,' said she.

'Scholars,' I finished briefly.

Miss Farington nodded. 'They will come,'
she said confidently, 'if the thing is properly
organised.'

Organisation was her hobby. If that little
affair came off, my library would be partly
catalogued and partly burnt, and To-to would

be organised into the stable-yard. Still I did not flinch.

'Think,' said she enthusiastically, 'what it would mean! To plant the first footing of knowledge, civilisation, refinement, among these peasants! To give them eyes to see the beauty of the nature which surrounds them! To give them resources for refined enjoyment when winter closes the door of nature to them! To widen their knowledge of the world, and teach them that "hinter den Bergen sind auch Leute!" Oh, Mr. Maude, if building and starting this school were to cost ten thousand pounds, I should say the money had been well spent if in it but one single Highland boy were taught to read!'

Rather appalled by the thought of the lengths to which such a boundless enthusiasm might carry her, I murmured something to the effect that it would be rather expensive. Whereat she turned upon me—

'And can you, Mr. Maude, who profess to revel in Montaigne and Shakespeare, delight in Charles Lamb and Alfred de Vigny, deny such pleasures to your humble neighbours?'

'But my humble neighbours wouldn't read Shakespeare or Montaigne, nor even Wilkie Collins nor Dumas the Elder. They'd read the *Bow Bells* novelettes. And as to teaching them to admire their own hills, why they love them more than you do, for Nature isn't to them a closed book in winter as it seems to you.'

I was on the wrong tack altogether, as I felt, when by good luck the lady herself brought me to more congenial ground.

'Then I suppose I mustn't expect much help from you, Mr. Maude,' she said, rather stiffly.

'Yes, you may indeed, you may expect every help,' I said, rushing at the opportunity, and growing hot over it. 'It's true I

—that—I don't much care—I mean I'm not deeply interested in Highland children, except as scenery, you know, picturesqueness and all that; but—er—but for you—in a plan of yours, that is to say, I should be delighted to do whatever lay in my power.'

During this lame performance Miss Farington listened with a perfectly stolid face, but with a heightened colour which told that she knew, in vulgar parlance, what I was driving at. Now that I was coming to the point, however, she did not mean to have any 'humbugging about.' At least, some such determination as that, rather than maiden coyness, seemed to prompt her next speech.

'I don't *think* I quite understand you, Mr. Maude.'

This was a challenge. I took it up.

'I think, Miss Farington, you must have noticed my growing interest in——'

'In my plans? No, indeed I haven't.

Don't you remember your saying the other day that it seemed a pity to waste good drainage and sanitary regulations upon people who were never ill ?'

' I—I only mean that my interest in—er —in drainage was swallowed up in my interest in you.'

It was the very last way in which I should have chosen to introduce a declaration of love, but with a girl too much absorbed in the progress of humanity to encourage that of the individual man, there is nothing for you but to take what opening you can get. It was all right, at any rate, for she smiled and gave me her hand, the glove of which I respectfully kissed, noticing at the time that it smelt of treacle, and wondering how it had acquired that particular perfume. It occurred to me, even as I stood there trying to think of something to say, that the little boys she had been teaching must have been eating

bread and treacle, and imparted its fragrance
to their lesson-books.

'You have surprised me very much, Mr.
Maude,' she said. 'Are you quite sure that
I deserve this honour?'

Perhaps the question was not so insincere
as it seemed to me, for she looked pleased,
though not at all agitated. But I felt, as I
reassured her with some conventional words,
that my heart would have gone out more to
the emptiest - headed little fool that ever
giggled and blushed than to this most intelligent and matter-of-fact young woman. And
I fell to wondering, as we began to walk
back together, why the sentimental and the
practical were so oddly divided in the feminine mind that a girl could glow with enthusiasm while talking about impracticable plans
for making her neighbours uncomfortable,
and listen quite coolly to a proposal to pass
her life with the man she had made no secret

of liking best. I had an awkward sense of
not knowing what to talk about, and I asked
her how she liked Larkhall. She had evidently considered that matter well already,
and was quite prepared with her answer.

'I think it only wants the south wing
raised a storey, and the drawing-room en-
larged by taking in that space between the
outer wall and that row of lilacs and guelder-
roses at the back, to make it one of the
pleasantest of the country houses about here,'
she replied promptly.

I felt a cold shiver up my back, perceiving that even my study might be already
doomed.

'But I like it even as it is because it is
your home,' she added, with a touch of human
feeling for which I felt grateful.

'Thank you,' I said, and I took her hand
again. I hesitated about using her Christian
name, and decided not to. 'Lucy' seemed

such an inappropriate appellation for Miss Farington ; she ought at least to have been ' Henrietta.'

' I will try to make you like it still more,' I said, quietly and sincerely, upon which she went the length of returning the pressure of my fingers on hers.

But she could not keep long away from those confounded plans. As we drew near the grounds of Larkhall, and could see the stables and one corner of the roof of the cottage, she stopped short and said pensively—

' I've often thought, Mr. Maude, what a pity it is that cottage should be kept empty, when it is so nicely furnished too. Your housekeeper, Mrs. Janet, took me over it one day.' Perhaps it was anger at the thought that this young lady had mentally disposed of all my property prematurely, perhaps annoyance that she should have intruded in the cottage at all, which helped to augment the sudden

fury which seized me at this suggestion. She
went on, quite unaware of what she had done.
' Now I was thinking what a charming convalescent home a place like that would make
for poor widows in reduced circumstances
who——'

'Unfortunately I am too selfish to give up
to strangers the accommodation which has
always been reserved for my friends.'

Miss Farington might be cold, might be
prosaic, but she was not stupid. She saw at
once she had gone too far, and hastened to
apologise with very maidenly humility.

'I am afraid you will think I care more
for my plans than for the great happiness and
honour you have just done me. But indeed,
Mr. Maude, it is not so. It is only that I
never find any one to sympathise with my
efforts but you, and so I tax your patience too
much in my delight at meeting some one who
is kind to me.'

'Be kind to me too, then,' I suggested, venturing, now that we had got among the trees of the garden, to put my hand lightly on her waist. She understood, and with a real blush at last, she let me kiss her. 'I have been a hermit a long time,' I said in a low voice, 'and I have fallen out of the ways of the world and of women. But if you will only have patience with me, and not be too much frightened by my uncouth ways, I will make you a very good husband; and I promise you it shall be your own fault if I do not make you happy.'

'I am sure of it,' she said simply, with a confidence which was flattering, if still astonishingly prosaic.

I led her round the garden, gathered for her my best roses and fastened them together, while she critically surveyed the front of the house.

'It wants a coat of whitewash, doesn't it?'

I suggested, anxious to show her that I was not too conservative.

'Ye—es, and the ivy wants trimming. Why don't you put it in the hands of the painters, Mr. Maude?'

'What, and go away—already! Surely that is too much to expect,' I ventured, looking down into her eyes, which, if not boasting any poetical attractions of 'hidden depths,' were very clear and straightforward.

'Oh no, I don't mean that; but you could come and stay nearer to us. The people at Lossie Villa are just going to leave, I know.'

'I am bound here for a little while, as one of my oldest friends has just asked me to give shelter to his wife and her mother for a few weeks.'

'Indeed! Oh, they will be some people to know. Have I ever heard of them?'

'I don't know. The mother's name is

Mrs. Ellmer, the daughter's—Mrs. Scott. She has been ill, I believe.'

'Mrs. Ellmer! Why, surely those are the people who used to live at the cottage! Oh, I have heard about them and your kindness to them. People said——' She hesitated.

'Well, what did they say?'

'Oh, well, they said you used to be very fond of—the daughter.'

'So I was; so I am. But you need not be jealous.'

She laughed, a bright clear laugh, scarcely without a touch of good-humoured contempt at the suggestion.

'I jealous! Oh, Mr. Maude, you would not seriously accuse me of such a paltry feeling! It would be unworthy of you, unworthy of me.'

I felt, when I had taken my *fiancée* home and formally received her parents' sanction

to our engagement, that I was myself unworthy to live in the intellectual and moral
heights on which she flourished. But I
could creep after her in a humble fashion,
and do my best to make her love me.

And in the meantime my loyalty to my
friend and my friend's wife was strengthened
by a new and sacred bond.

CHAPTER XXI

I SUPPOSE no man ever tried harder to be deeply, earnestly, sincerely in love than I tried to be with Miss Farington ; and I suppose no man ever failed more completely. I believe now that to any other woman I have ever met, being a man by no means without affectionate impulses, and being also in a most propitious mood for sentiment, I should have been by the end of the week a submissive if not adoring slave. I wanted to be a slave ; I was even anxious to become, for the time at least, the mere chattel of somebody else, a gracious and kindly somebody, be it well understood, who would give me

the wages of affection in return for my best
efforts in her service.

But Miss Farington's heart and mind were
far too well regulated for her to tolerate, much
less seek, such an empire over the man who
was to be her lord and master.   She despised
sentiment, and meant to begin as she intended
to keep on, neither giving nor accepting an
unreasonable amount of affection.   Respect
and esteem, and above all, compatibility of
aim, she used to say, not harshly, but with an
implied reproach to my own more vulgar and
sensual views, were the only sure foundation
of happy married life ; and I felt that so long
as there was an unrepaired pig-stye within a
mile of Larkhall, I was an object of compara-
tively small importance in my *fiancée's* eyes.
And the worst of it was I couldn't contradict
her.   Reserving all her philanthropic pro-
jects, she was on other matters the incarnation of common sense ; and I soon found that

it was the vague reputation for intellect which any man gets in the country who likes his books better than his neighbours, which had attracted her attention to my unworthy self. She was disappointed with her bargain already ; I was sure of that : but having made it, she was not the woman to go back from her word. She even had the good taste, on finding that her 'plans' palled upon me, to drop them out of her conversation to a great extent, but I had a shrewd suspicion that they would be let loose upon me again with full force as soon as she should be installed as mistress of Larkhall. I was secretly resolved however, since my lady-love declined to rule me in the right woman's way—through her heart—to assert my supremacy of the head in a startling and unexpected manner so soon as I should be legally the master.

In the meantime we jogged on with our engagement, and I found in my daily walks with Lucy, and in luncheons and teas at her father's, no charm strong enough to make me for a moment forget the fact that in a few days Babiole would be under my own roof.

For I had decided that not honour enough could be done to my guests at the cottage; and, Ferguson and old Janet joining in the work with a heartiness which made me love them, we turned out the whole house from garret to basement, and for a week there was such a sweeping and garnishing as never was known. We had only just got it in order when Fabian's telegram came announcing that they were off, and for the next forty-eight hours nobody could stop to take breath. The stable-boy had insisted on erecting at the entrance a lop-sided triumphal arch which, after having required constant renewing of its branches for a day and a half, having been put up much too soon, had to be taken down at the last moment, as it was found that a carriage could not drive under it without either the arch carrying away the coachman, or the coachman carrying away the arch. They were to break the journey by spending one night at Edinburgh, and I had proposed to meet them at Aberdeen on the following day. But Miss Farington's uncle having come to Ballater on purpose to annoy me—I mean on purpose to meet me—I was forced to attend a most dull luncheon at Oak Lodge where I, in absence of mind, made myself very objectionable by expressing a doubt whether any lawyers would be found in heaven.

They made me stay to tea, though I'm sure nobody wanted me, and I was dying to get away. It was nearly six before I could leave, and I rushed to the little station just as the passengers were streaming out of the train. I knew that Babiole was among them, and I came upon her suddenly as I got through the

door on to the platform. She was leaning
on her mother, pale, thin, wasted so that for
pity and terror I could not speak, but just
held out my arm and supported her to the
carriage which, by my orders, was waiting outside. As we drove off she leaned
against her mother and held out her hand
to me.

'Again—after four years, to be back with
you under old Craigendarroch,' she said,
almost in a whisper, with moist eyes.

'Yes, yes, we'll set you up again as none
of your London doctors could do,' I said
huskily.

She smiled at me, still keeping my hand.

'Will you, Mr. Maude?' she asked half
doubtingly, like a child.

'See what marriage has done for her!'
broke in Mrs. Ellmer half mournfully, half
tartly. 'She wouldn't be satisfied till she'd
tried it, and look at the result.'

At that moment a yelping and barking behind us attracted our attention, and the next moment poor old Ta-ta, released from the van in which she had been travelling, overtook the carriage, and tried to leap up from the road to lick my face.

'Ta-ta, old girl, why, we're going to have the old times back again,' I cried, much moved; and after a drive in which only Mrs. Ellmer talked much, we all reached Larkhall in a more or less maudlin condition, overcome by old recollections.

All the men and boys about the place had assembled in two rows at the entrance, and gave us a hearty cheer as we drove past. Ferguson was standing at the door, and I vow his hard old eyes were moist as he insisted on helping the little lady out himself. Janet, in a cap which rendered the wearer insignificant, made a respectful curtsey to Mrs. Scott as she came up the steps, but threw her arms around her as soon as she was fairly inside the hall.

Mrs. Ellmer and I were rather afraid of the effects of fatigue and excitement on a frame scarcely convalescent, but the pleasure of being back among the hills was such a powerful stimulant that within half an hour of going upstairs to the big south bedroom, which had been aired and cleaned and done up expressly for her, she flitted down again with quick steps, and with a faint stain of pink colour showing under the transparent skin of her thin cheeks.

I was just outside the front door, where I had been hovering about with an unlighted cigar between my lips, when I caught a glimpse of soft white drapery in the heavy shadows of the old staircase. I went back into the hall and looked up at her, as she stopped with one hand on the bannisters, smiling down at me but saying nothing.

She wore a transparent white dress that looked like muslin only that it was silky, with a long train that remained stretched on the stairs above her as she stopped.

'I thought it was an angel flying over my staircase,' I said gently.

'And all the while it was only a silly moth that had singed its wings in the big bright candle you had warned it to keep away from,' she answered gravely, after a pause.

'The wings will grow again, and when it goes back to the light——'

'We won't talk about going back yet,' she broke in with a little shiver. 'I want to forget all about London for a little while, and try to feel just as I used to do here. I wouldn't bring Davis with me. Poor mamma is going to be my nurse, and you to be my doctor, and I am going to take Craigendarroch after every meal.'

'You must be ready for one now, one

meal, I mean, not one mountain. Where is poor mamma?'

'Oh, she's gone to talk to Janet. She thinks I am still waiting for her to do my hair. But she shall see that I am not an invalid any longer.'

But as she spoke, the light died out of her eyes, and I saw the fragile white hand, the blue-veined delicacy of which had alarmed me, suddenly clutch the bannister-rail tightly.

'You mustn't boast too soon,' said I, as I ran up the stairs and supported her.

She recovered herself in a few moments, being only very weak and tired, and she suddenly lifted her face to mine quite merrily.

'Shall we take Froude to-morrow, Mr. Maude? Or shall I prepare a chapter of Schiller's *Thirty Years' War?*' she asked, just in the old manner. 'Or a couple of pages of *Ancient History?*'

'I think,' I answered slowly, while my heart leapt up as a salmon does at a fly, and I honestly tried not to feel so disloyally, unmistakably happy, 'that we'll do a little modern poetry, and that we'll begin with " The Return of the Wanderer."'

I was leading her slowly downstairs, when Mrs. Ellmer's high piercing voice, coming towards us as the door of the housekeeper's room was opened, suddenly broke upon our ears.

'Well, I must go and congratulate him. I'm sure I always said that a nice wife was just the one thing he wanted.'

'Who's that?' asked Babiole quite sharply.

'Why, don't you know your own mother's voice?'

'Yes, yes, but who is she talking about? Who is it wants a nice wife?'

'I suppose most of us do, only we are not all so lucky as a certain young actor I know,'

I said brightly; but my heart beat violently,
and I felt Babiole's fingers trembling on my
arm.

She asked me no more questions, and I
took her into the dining-room to admire the
roses with which we had loaded the table.
But when her mother joined us a moment
later, brimming over with excitement about
my engagement, Babiole nodded and said,
'Yes, mother, I've heard all about it,' and
offered no congratulations.

As for me, the remembrance of my
fiancée this evening threw me into a reckless
mood. 'Let us eat and drink, for to-morrow
we — marry Miss Farington' was the kind
of thought that lay at the bottom of my
deliberate abandonment of myself to the
enthralling pleasure the mere presence of
this little white human thing had power to
give me. Mrs. Ellmer and I were very
lively both at dinner and afterwards in the

study, where we all went merely to look at To-to, but where Babiole insisted on our staying. She did not talk much ; but on the other hand, her face never for a moment fell into that listless sadness which had pained and shocked me so much in London. When at last she was so evidently tired out that we had reluctantly to admit that she must go to bed, she let her mother see that she wanted to speak to me, and remained behind to say—

'I want to see this lady you are going to marry. For I'm not going to congratulate you till I see whether she is sweet, and beautiful, and noble, and worthy to—worship you, Mr. Maude,' she ended earnestly.

'She is a very nice girl,' said I, playing with To-to with unconscious roughness, which the monkey resented.

'A nice girl for *you !* ' she said scornfully. 'She must be more than that, or I will forbid the banns. I was afraid you would think it

strange that I didn't say something about it,'
she went on, after a moment's pause, rather
nervously; 'but when I heard it—just now—
I prayed about it—I did indeed—just as I
used to for myself and Fabian.'

A fear evidently struck her here that the
reminiscence was ill-omened, for she hastened
to add, 'But then I didn't deserve to be
happy—and you do. Good-night,' she concluded abruptly, and drawing her hot hand
with nervous haste out of mine she left me.

The next day came a reaction from the
excitement of her arrival, and Babiole was
not able to leave her room until late in the
afternoon. I had paid my duty-call at Oak
Lodge in the morning, and had been dis-
concerted to find that common sense and
philanthropy had grown less attractive than
ever. Lucy expressed her intention of calling upon Mrs. Scott that very afternoon, and
when I explained that she was tired and not

likely to make her appearance before dinner-
time, my philanthropist said she would drive
round to Larkhall in the evening. From
this pertinacity I concluded that Miss
Farington was perhaps not so entirely free
from human curiosity and perhaps feminine
jealousy as she would have liked me to
suppose. At any rate she kept me with her
all day, an unquiet conscience having made
me exceedingly docile; and it was six o'clock
before I got home.

I went straight into the drawing-room,
where Babiole, lying on a sofa before one of
the windows, was enjoying the warm light of
the declining sun.

'Better?' said I simply, coming up to the
sofa and looking down. All the energy and
animation of the evening before were gone
now; but to me Babiole never lost one
charm without gaining a greater; she had
been fascinating in a lively mood, she was

irresistible in a quiet one. She gave me
her hand and answered in a weak voice—

'Yes, I'm better, thank you.'

'What have you been thinking about so
quietly all by yourself? I don't fancy you
ought to be allowed to think at all.'

'I've been thinking about poor papa.
Have you heard anything more about him?'

'Yes, he's all right, I believe, settled
down in Aberdeen. I don't think you'd
better try to see him though. It might set
him worrying again on the old subject,
which perhaps he has forgotten.'

She shook her head. 'You don't know
papa as mamma and I do. He wastes his life
so that people despise him, and believe that
he cares for nothing but the day's enjoyment.
But they are wrong. He is fierce and sullen,
and he never forgets. He came up here to
see *you*, and to do you harm ; and he will
never rest until at least he's tried to.'

'Well, he and I were very good friends, and there is nothing I should like better than to meet him and make him listen to reason—as I'm sure he would do.'

'He—he might not give you the chance.'

I was pleased by her solicitude for me, but I showed her how very far-fetched her fears were, and assured her, moreover, that if Mr. Ellmer, with the brutal ferocity which had been ascribed to him, should ever go so far as to attack me personally, he would probably find his match in a man who lived so hardily as I.

CHAPTER XXII

I DID not mention Miss Farington's
threatened visit until the very moment
when, after dinner, as we were all turning
out for a walk round the garden, I caught a
glimpse of her little pony carriage between
the trees of the drive. Babiole, wrapt in a
long shawl of Indian embroidery which I had
taken a fancy to in a bazaar in Calcutta, and
had sent home to her, was standing by a
rose-tree and choosing the flowers which I
was to cut. Mrs. Ellmer, with characteristic
vivacity, was running little races with old
Ta-ta, whose failing energy was now satisfied
with such small performances as these. The

dog stopped short to bark at the carriage, to which Mrs. Ellmer now directed my attention.

'Oh yes, it's Miss Farington, I think; she said she might come round this evening.'

'What! Miss Farington? Your young lady? And you could forget that she was coming! Oh, naughty, naughty!' cried Mrs. Ellmer.

Babiole's face had flushed from chin to forehead.

'We must go and meet her,' she said quietly, setting the example of going up the steps which led from terrace to terrace to the house.

Reminded of my duty, I hastened up to the lawn, and was just in time to help my visitor out of the little carriage. She wore a gray dress, a dark blue jacket, a brown hat, and black silk gloves—a costume in which I had seen her often before, but which had not struck me as being a hideous combination until I saw it straightway after looking at a figure which, seen in the soft evening shadows which had begun to creep up under the trees, had left in my mind an intoxicating vision of rich colours and soft outlines, like the conception of an Indian princess by an Impressionist painter.

Lucy Farington's manner suffered as much by contrast with Mrs. Scott's as her dress had done. Never before had she seemed so matter-of-fact, so brusque, so blind and deaf to everything that was not strictly useful or severely intellectual. On finding that Mrs. Scott took but a tepid interest in the subject of artisans' dwellings, and had no acquaintance with the writings either of Kant or Klopstock, she glanced at me, who had never been bold enough to avow the whole depth of my indifference to the one and my ignorance of the other subject, with an expression of scarcely disguised contempt.

'I'm afraid Henry and I shall scarcely find in you a warm sympathiser with our plans, Mrs. Scott,' she said with rather a pitying smile. 'But of course we must not expect you London ladies to condescend to take an interest in cottagers; and it is only we poor country girls who, for want of anything better to do, have to improve our minds.'

We were all in the drawing-room now, to my great regret, for I felt that if we had remained in the garden we might have dispersed ourselves, and I might have been spared hearing my *fiancée's* unaccountable outbreak of bad taste. Babiole answered very quietly.

'You have misunderstood me a little, I am afraid, Miss Farington,' she said. 'It is not that my mother and I don't take an *interest* in cottagers; but that, having been cottagers ourselves, and having known and visited cottagers rather as friends than as patrons, we can't at once jump into the habit of considering them wholesale, as if we were poor-law guardians.'

'And as for improving one's mind,' broke in Mrs. Ellmer, who was growing exceedingly irate at the persistent manner in which the philanthropist ignored her, 'you must blame Mr. Maude if she is not learned enough, for it was he who educated her.'

This bold speech made a great sensation. Miss Farington drew herself up. Babiole shot at me an eloquent involuntary glance from eyes which were suddenly filled with tears; while I confess that if I had been called upon to speak at that moment I should have gone near to choking. In the meantime Mrs. Ellmer went on undaunted.

'I suppose it's very old-fashioned to think that one's studies ought to be with the object of giving pleasure to other people. But I'm sure it's pleasanter to hear a girl play a nice piece of music than to hear her talk about books that most of us have never heard of.'

'I love music—*good* music,' said Lucy coldly. 'No study is more refining and more profound than that of the great masters of harmony. I had no idea, Mrs. Scott, that you were an accomplished amateur. Will you not give me the pleasure of hearing you?'

'I am afraid I am not a very scientific student,' said Babiole, as she walked towards the piano, which I opened for her.

She looked so pale and tired that I suggested in a low voice that she had better not play to-night. She glanced at Miss Farington, however, and I, following the direction of her eyes, saw that my *fiancée* was watching us in a displeased manner. I therefore beat a retreat from the piano, and Babiole began to play. She was a good performer, and though not one of phenomenal accomplishment, she seemed to me to give something of her own grace and charm to the music she interpreted. She was nervous this evening on account of the critical element in the audience; but I thought she played with even more of sympathy and of power than usual. She had chosen one of the less hackneyed of Mendelssohn's 'Songs without Words,' and when she had finished I thanked her heartily, while Miss Farington chimed in with more reserve.

'I am afraid,' said Babiole, 'that it is not the sort of music to give you great pleasure, but I can't play much by heart, and that is one of the few things I know.'

'Of course,' agreed Miss Farington readily, 'I acquit you of such a terrible charge as an enthusiasm for the shallow sentimentalism of the "Lieder ohne Worte." Some day, I hope, in the day-time, you will let me have the pleasure of hearing you play

something you really like.   It is really very
good of you to have received me at all so
late, but I had heard so much about you that
I really must plead guilty to the *childish*
charge of not being able to control my impatience to see you.'

And Miss Farington took leave of the
two ladies and sailed out of the room, followed
meekly by me.   I was in no affectionate
mood, having been astonished and disgusted
by her undreamt-of powers of making herself
disagreeable.

' I want you to come and spend the day
at Oak Lodge to-morrow, Henry,' she said
in a kinder tone than she had used during
the evening, as soon as she was seated in the
pony-carriage.   ' I have some designs of a
new church to show you, which I think even
you will like ; and my Uncle Matthew is
most anxious to see more of you than he had
a chance of doing yesterday.'

'Thank you; it is very kind,' I answered rather coldly; 'and of course I shall be happy to come and see you to-morrow as usual if you will let me. But I couldn't spend the whole day at Oak Lodge, because, you see, I have guests to consider.'

'And can't they spare you for a single afternoon?' asked Lucy with a hard laugh. 'I shall really begin to feel quite jealous.'

'You need not indeed,' I broke out hastily and earnestly, 'I assure you——'

She interrupted me in a very abrupt and icy manner. 'Pray do not take the trouble. No man who was such a flimsy creature as to give me reason for jealousy could possibly retain a hold upon my affections.'

'Of course not,' I assented, in my usual mean-spirited way, but with a dawning suspicion that my *fiancée's* affections would not prove strong enough for even a less flimsy creature than I to obtain a firm grip on.

'My father and Mrs. Farington will drive over to-morrow,' Lucy went on; 'I believe they intend to ask Mrs. Scott to dinner. I suppose one must ask the mother too,' she added dubiously.

'It will certainly be better, unless you wish to insult them both,' I said in an unnaturally subdued tone the significance of which I think she failed to notice. 'But in any case the invitation will have no awful results, for Mrs. Scott is not well enough to go out to dinners.'

'Ah, poor thing, I suppose not. She looks very ill. It seems almost impossible to believe what they tell me, that she was once very pretty. Perhaps she would not look so bad though if somebody could only persuade her to dress like other people. Did you ever see anything like that shawl arrangement she had on when I first came?'

'Never,' said I calmly. 'But I confess I am barbarous enough to think that a merit.

Every lady's style of dress should have something unique about it.'

'Indeed!   Then how about mine?'

'Your style of dress is unique too,' said I
politely.

Miss Farington looked at me doubtfully,
but came, I think, to the conclusion that she
had been disagreeable enough for one day,
even if this compliment were a dubious one.
So she contented herself with begging me
warmly to come early the next day and to
remember that my guests were not to absorb
me too entirely, and then she advanced her
cheek for me to kiss and drove away through
the trees. When I turned back into the house
I found a great turmoil prevailing. 'Mistress Scott had been on her way to her room
when she had swooned awa' on the stairs,'
Janet said.   I stole presently up the staircase
to her door, and Mrs. Ellmer came out to
tell me that Babiole had indeed been over-

come by fatigue and had fainted, but that she was much better now, and would be all right in the morning after the night's rest.

But I was anxious about the poor child; for her pallor during the evening had frightened me. My Lucy's new departure too had given me something to think about, so that sleep for the present was out of the question. I therefore determined to keep my vigil comfortably; going into the study, I threw another log on the fire which, winter and summer, was always necessary in the evening, and, lighting my pipe, stretched myself in my old chair and gave myself up to meditation, which resolved itself before long into a doze.

I woke up suddenly before the fire had got low, and heard the old boards of the floor above me creaking repeatedly, as if some one were hurrying about on them with a soft tread. The room over my study was that which had been assigned to Mrs. Scott, so that I was on the alert at once, afraid that she had been taken ill again in the night, and that her mother, who slept in a little room next to hers, was running to and fro in attendance upon her.

I jumped up from my chair, with the intention of going upstairs to ask Mrs. Ellmer whether I could be of any use ; but before I had taken two steps, in a slow sleepy fashion, listening all the time, the creaking ceased, and I heard the sound of a door being opened on the landing above. The study-door was ajar, so that in the complete stillness of the night the faintest noise was audible to me. I crossed the room softly, creeping nearer to the door with keenly open ears and with something more than curiosity in my mind. For without being at all one of those highly sensitive persons who can distinguish without fail one footfall from another, I knew the

difference between Mrs. Ellmer's quick active
step, and the slow soft tread which I now
heard on the polished uncarpeted floor of the
corridor. The steps became inaudible as I
caught the light sound of a skirt sweeping
from stair to stair : then again I heard a slow
tread on the polished floor of the hall. Although I knew well enough who it was, a long
sigh which suddenly reached my ears and
proclaimed beyond doubt the wanderer's
identity, seemed to pierce my body and leave
a deep wound. It was Babiole, either in
misery or in pain, who was wandering about
the house in the middle of the night. She
was feeling about for something in the darkness when I opened wide the door of my
study, and let the lamplight fall upon her just
as the chain of the front door rattled in her
hands and fell with a loud noise against the oak.

She glanced back at me in a startled manner, but proceeded to unlock the door and to

turn the handle.   She had on the muslin
dress she had worn during the evening, with
her travelling cloak and bonnet.   I saw by
the vacant manner in which her eyes rested
for a moment upon me, without surprise or
recognition, that there was some cloud in her
brain.   I advanced quickly into the hall and
laid my fingers upon the handle of the door.

'What are you doing down here to-night?'
I asked in a low voice, but with an air of
authority.   'You ought to be sleeping.'

She drew back a little and looked helplessly from the door to me.

'Now go upstairs again and get into bed
as fast as you can,' I continued coaxingly, 'or
your mother will find out that you have left
your room, and be very much frightened.'

But recalling her purpose, she made a
spring towards the door, and as I stood firm
and prevented her opening it, she fell to wild
and piteous entreaties.

'Let me pass, please. I must go, I tell you I must go, before they know—before they guess. It will all come right if I go.'

'Tell me first why you want to go,' said I gently.

The lamp-light streamed out from the open study door upon us, showing me her dazed, almost haggard face, her disordered dress, the nervous trembling of her hands. She looked at me for a moment more steadily, and I thought she was coming to herself.

'I can't tell *you*,' she whispered, still fumbling with the door handle and looking down at her own fingers.

'Well, then, go upstairs now, and you shall tell me all about it to-morrow,' I said persuasively.

'No, no, no,' she broke out wildly and vehemently as at first, seeming again to lose all control of herself as she became excited. 'To-morrow I shall be happy again, and I shall

not be able to go.   He cannot care for this
girl while I'm here, I know it!   I am spoiling everything for them : I want to go back
to my husband, and not wait for him to come
and fetch me.   Don't you see ?   Don't you
understand ? '

Even while she babbled out these secrets,
ignorant who I was, her instinct of confidence
in me made her support herself on my arm,
and lean upon me as she whispered excitedly
in my ear.

'Well, but it is night, and there are no
trains till the morning, you know.'

For a moment she seemed bewildered.
Then with an expression of childlike sim-
plicity she said, 'I shall find my way.   God
told me I was right to go.   I can pray up
here among the hills, just as I used when I
was a child, and He told me it was right.'

Luckily, perhaps, her strength was failing
her even as she spoke.   She swayed unsteadily

on my arm and made little resistance but a
faint murmur of protest as I half carried her
back to the staircase.   As her head fell
languidly against my shoulder I saw that
again, as fatigue overcame excitement, she
was recovering her wandering consciousness,
and I made haste to take advantage of the
fact.

'Come,' said I, 'you had better go upstairs
and rest a little while—before you start, you
know.'

She looked up at me in a dreamy bewildered manner as she leant, supported by my
arms, against the staircase, and two tears,
shining in the darkness, rolled down her
cheeks.   'I am afraid,' said she in a broken
whisper, 'that I shall not be able to go at all.'

Then, with a long sigh, she stood up,
twined her arms within mine and let me lead
her upstairs.   The door of her room was
open, and the two candles, flickering and

smoking in the draught, cast moving shadows over a disorder of dress and dainty woman's clothing flung in confusion about the room. Babiole glanced inside and then looked up at me in bewilderment and alarm, like one roused out of sleep to see something strange and terrible. I wanted her to go to rest before her memory should overtake her. So I took off her bonnet and cloak, and profiting by the utter docility she showed me, glanced into the room and said, in a tone of authority, such as one would use to a child—

'Now, I shall come upstairs again in exactly five minutes and shall knock at your door. If you are in bed by that time you are to call out "good-night." If you are not, I shall wake your mother up, and send her to you. Now will you do as I tell you?'

'Yes, yes,' said she meekly.

'Then good-night.'

'Good-night, Mr. Maude.'

She knew me then; but I somehow fancied, from the old-fashioned demureness with which she gave her hand, that she believed herself to be once more the little maid of Craigendarroch, and me to be her old master.

Next day Babiole did not appear at breakfast, and her mother said she was in a state of deep depression, and must, her mother thought by her manner, have had a fright in the night. I was very anxious to see her again, and to find out how much she remembered of our nocturnal adventure. So anxious was I, in fact, that I forgot all about my appointment at Oak Lodge at eleven, and it was not until Mrs. Ellmer and I were having luncheon at two that I was suddenly reminded of my neglect in a rather summary fashion by being presented by Ferguson with a note directed in my *fiancée's* handwriting, and told that a messenger was waiting. I

opened it, conscience-stricken, but hardly
prepared for the blow it contained.   This
was the note :—

'DEAR MR. MAUDE—' [The opening was por-
tentous] 'It is with feelings of acute pain that I
address thus formally a gentleman in whom I once
thought I had had the good fortune to discover a
heart, and more especially a mind, to which I
could in all things submit the control of my own
weaker and more frivolous nature.' [Lucy Farington frivolous !   Shades of Aristotle and Bacon !]
'For some time past I have begun to feel that I
was deceived.   I do not for a moment mean that
you intended deception, but that, in my anxiety
to believe the best, I deceived myself.   Your
growing indifference to the dearest wishes of my
heart, culminating in your positive non-appearance
this morning (when I had prepared a little surprise
for you in shape of a meeting with Mr. Finch,
the architect, with his designs for a model self-
supporting village laundry), leave hardly any
room for doubt that our views of life are too hopelessly dissimilar for us to hope to embark happily
in matrimony.   If this is indeed the case, with

much regret I will give you back your liberty, and request the return of my perhaps foolishly fond letters. If, on the other hand, you are not willing that all should be at an end between us, I beg that you will come to me in the pony carriage which will await your orders.—I remain, dear Mr. Maude, with my sincerest apologies if I have been unduly hasty, yours most sincerely,

'LUCY FARINGTON.'

My first emotion was one of anger against the girl for being such a fool ; my second was of thankfulness to her for being so wise. I should have liked, in pique, to have straight-way got those letters, which she was mistaken in considering compromisingly affectionate, to have made them into a small but neat parcel and despatched them forthwith. In-stead of this, I excused myself to Mrs. Ellmer, went into the study in a state of excitement, half pain and half relief, and wrote a note.

'MY DEAR MISS FARINGTON—Your letter forbids me to address you in a more affectionate

way, though you are mistaken in supposing that
my feelings towards you have changed. It seems
to be that we have both, if I may use the expression, been running our heads against a brick wall.
You have been seeking in me a learned gentleman with a strong natural bent for philanthropy,
while I hoped to find in you an intelligent and
withal most kind and loving-hearted girl, who
would condescend to console me for the "slings
and arrows of outrageous fortune," in return for
my very best endeavours to make her happy.
Well, is the mistake past repairing? I am not
too old to learn philanthropy under your guidance ;
you, I am sure, are too sweet not to forgive me
for preferring a walk with you alone to interviews
with all the architects who ever desecrated nature.
I cannot come back with the carriage now to see
Mr. Finch ; but if you will, in the course of the
afternoon, let me have another ever so short note
telling me to come and see *you*, I shall take it
as a token that you are willing to give me another
chance, and within half an hour of receiving it I
will be with you to take my first serious lesson in
philanthropy and to pay for it in what love coin
you please.—Believe me, dear Lucy if I may,

dear Miss Farington if I must, yours ever most faithfully and sincerely,

'HENRY L. MAUDE.'

I saw the groom drive off with this note, and spent the early part of the afternoon wandering about the garden, trying to make out what sort of answer I wished for. This was the one I got :—

'DEAR MR. MAUDE—The tone of levity which characterises your note admits but of one explanation. No gentleman could so address the lady whose respect and esteem he sincerely wished to retain. I therefore return your letters and the various presents you have been kind enough to make me, and beg that you will return me my share of our correspondence. Please do not think I bear you any ill-will ; I am willing to believe the error was mutual, and shall rather increase than discontinue my prayers on your behalf, that your perhaps somewhat pliable nature may not render you the victim of designing persons.— I remain, dear Mr. Maude, ever sincerely your friend,   LUCY FARINGTON.'

When I got to the end of this warm-hearted effusion I rushed off to make up my parcel : seven notes, a smoking-cap, and a pair of slippers, which last I regretted giving up, as they were large and comfortable; a book on Village Architecture, and another of sermons by an eloquent and unpractical modern preacher, completed the list. I fastened them up, sealed and directed them, and sent them out to the under-gardener from 'Oak Lodge,' who had brought the note, and had been directed to wait for an answer. Then, with a sense of relief which was un-mixed this time, I went back to my study, lit my pipe, and sat down in front of the parcel my late love had sent me. I was struck by its enormous superiority in neatness to the ill-shapen brown paper bundle in which I had just sent off mine ; and it presently occurred to me that the remarkable deftness with which corners had been turned in and string knotted and tied could never have been attained by hands unused to any kind of active labour. Miss Farington, either too much overcome by emotion to tie her parcel up herself, or from an absence of sentiment which might or might not be considered to do her credit, had entrusted the task of sending back my presents to her maid.

Mechanically I opened the parcel and, not being deeply enough wounded by the abrupt termination of my engagement to throw my rejected gifts with passion into the fire, I arranged them on the table in a row, spread out my returned letters (which had all been neatly opened with a pen—or small paper-knife), and considered the well-meant but disastrous venture of which they were the relics with much thoughtfulness. It had been a failure from first to last: not only had it failed to draw my thoughts and affections from the little pale lady who was now the

wife of my friend, but it had also unhappily
resulted in rendering her by contrast a love-
lier and more desirable object than before.
There was no doubt of it : the only unalloyed
pleasure my *fiancée* had afforded me was the
increase of delight I had felt, after nearly
three weeks of her improving society, in
meeting my little witch of the hills once more.
On the whole my conscience was pretty clear
with regard to Miss Farington ; I had been
prepared to offer her affection, and she had
preferred an interest in domestic architecture,
which I had then sedulously cultivated : the
question was, what was to be done now ?   I
decided that the most prudent course would
be to say nothing of my rupture with my
lady-love, and if I should be unable to subdue
a certain unwonted hilarity at dinner time, to
ascribe it to other causes.

I had scarcely made this resolution, however, when I heard light sounds in the hall

and a knock at my door, and I said 'Come in' with my heart leaping up and a hot and feverish conviction that it was all up with the secret; for the outspread letters which I convulsively gathered into a heap, the lace pocket-handkerchief, the chased gold smelling-bottle, and other articles for which a bachelor of retired habits would be likely to have small use, told their own tale; while, to make matters worse, To-to had got hold of the engagement ring and had placed it on the top of his box for safety while he minutely inspected its morocco case, and chewed up the velvet lining with all the zest of a gourmand.

One helpless glance was all I had time for before the door opened, and Babiole came in.

CHAPTER XXIII

On hearing the soft tap of Babiole's fingers
on the door of my study, there had sprung up
in me quite suddenly a feeling that my anchor
was gone, and the tempest of human passion
which I had controlled for so long burst out
within me with a violence which made me
afraid of myself. There, on the table before
me, lay the eloquent relics of my rejected
suit to the woman I had tried to love. And
here, shut out from me only by the scarcely-
closed door, was the woman I loved so dearly
without the trying, that just that faint sound
which told me she was near thrilled through
every fibre of my body as the musician's

careless fingers sweep the keys of his instru-
ment in a lightly-touched prelude before he
makes it sing and throb with any melody he
pleases. I had sprung to my feet and begun
to toss my returned letters one by one with
shaking hands into the fire, when I heard
Babiole's voice behind me.

I turned abruptly, and it seemed to myself
almost defiantly. But no sooner had I
given one glance at the slender figure dressed
in some plain dark stuff and one into the little
pale face than all the tumult within me began
to calm down, and the roaring, ramping,
raging lion I had felt a moment before trans-
formed himself gradually before the unconscious magic of my fairy's eyes into the mild
and meek old lamb he had always been with
her.

'You seem very busy, Mr. Maude,' said
she, smiling.

Surely it was my very witch herself again,

only a little thinner and whiter, who spoke to
me thus in the old sweet voice, and held out
her hand with the half-frank, half-shy demureness of those bygone, painful-pleasant days
when we were 'engaged,' and when the new
and proud discovery that she was 'grown-up'
had given a delicious piquancy to her manner
of taking her lessons! I shook hands with
her, and she pointed to her old chair; as she
took it quite simply and thus had the full
light of the windows on her face, I noticed
with surprise and pleasure that, in spite of the
excitement of the night before, the atmosphere of her old home was already taking
effect upon her, the listless expression she had
worn in London was disappearing from her
face, and the old child-like look which blue
eyes were meant to wear was coming back
into them again.

'You are better,' said I gently, taking no
notice of her remark upon my occupation.

'You have been lazy, madam. I am sure
you might very well have come down to
breakfast. You had a good night, I suppose ?'

Ta-ta, who had followed her into the room,
pushed her nose lovingly into her old companion's hand, and Babiole hid a sensitively
flushing face by bending low over the dog's
sleek head. I think she must have found
out that morning by the confusion in her room
that something had happened the night before, the details of which she could not remember; perhaps also she had a vague
remembrance of her expedition downstairs,
and wanted to find out what I knew about it.
But of course I knew nothing.

'Yes, I—I slept well—thank you. Only I
had dreams.'

'Did you? Not bad ones, I hope ?'

She glanced at me penetratingly, but
could discover nothing, as I was fighting with

To-to over the fragments of the morocco ring case.

'No-o, not exactly bad, but very strange. Do you know—I found—my travelling hat and cloak—lying about—and I wondered whether—in my sleep—I had put them on —thinking I was—going back to London!'

All this, uttered very slowly and with much hesitation, I listened to without interruption, and then, standing up with my back to the fire, nodded to her reassuringly.

'Well, so you did, Mrs. Scott, and a nice fright your sleep-walking propensities gave me, I can tell you. It was by the luckiest chance in the world that I didn't brain you with the poker for a burglar when I heard footsteps in the hall in the middle of the night!'

'You did!' cried she, pale to the lips with apprehension.

'Yes; and when I saw you, you muttered

something I couldn't understand, and then you half woke up, and you went back quickly to your room again, leaving me considerably wider awake than before.'

'Is that all?' asked Babiole, the faint colour coming back to her face again.

'It was quite enough for me, I assure you. And I hope you will take your walking exercise for the future in the day-time, when my elderly nerves are at their best.'

Babiole laughed, much relieved. She evidently retained such a vivid impression of the thoughts which had preyed upon her excited mind on the previous evening that she was tormented by the fear or the dim remembrance of having given them expression. She now looked with awakening interest at the odd collection on the table.

'Are you making preparations for a fancy bazaar, Mr. Maude?' she asked, taking up a case which contained a gold thimble.

But she knew what the exhibition meant, and she was glad, though neither of us looked at the other as she put this question, and I made my answer.

'No; the bazaar is over, and these are the things left on my hands.'

'Then I am afraid—the bazaar—has not been very successful?' she hazarded playfully, but in a rather unsteady voice.

'Not very. My customers were discontented with their bargain, and wanted their money back.'

Babiole's sensitive face flushed suddenly with hot indignation.

'How dare she——' she began passionately, and stopped.

'My dear Mrs. Scott, these girls dare anything!' said I lightly, in high spirits at the warmth with which she took up my cause. 'There is no respect left for the superior sex now that ladies out-read us, out-write us, out-

shoot us, and out-fish us.   And the end of it
is that I wash my hands of them, and have
made up my mind to die a bachelor!'

If she could have known how clearly her
fair eyes showed me every succeeding emotion of her heart and thought of her brain, as
I glanced with apparent carelessness at her
face while I spoke, she would have died of
shame.   I had thought, on that night when
I met her in London when she had charmed
and yet pained me by her brilliant, graceful,
but somewhat artificial manner, that she was
changed, that I should have to learn my
Babiole over again.   But it was only the
pretty little closed doors I had seen outside
her shut-up heart.   When the heart was
called to, the doors flew open, and here
was the treasure exposed again to every
touch, so that I had read in her mobile
face indignation, affection, jealousy, sympathy, and finally contentment, before she

remarked in a very demure and indifferent manner—

'On the whole I am not sorry, Mr. Maude, that it is broken off. She wasn't half good enough for you.'

'Not good enough for me?' I cried in affected surprise. I was thirsting for her pretty praises. 'I'm sure everybody who knew me thought me a very lucky man.'

'Nobody who knew both well could have thought that,' she answered very quietly. 'Wasn't she rude to mamma, whom you treated as if she were a queen? Is she not hard and overbearing in her manner to you, who have offered her the greatest honour you could give? And wasn't she, for all the cold charity she prides herself upon, distant and contemptuous to me when she knew I had been the object of *your* charity for seven years?'

'Not charity, child——'

'Oh, but it was.   Charity that was real,
full of heart and warmth and kindness, that
made the world a new place and life a new
thing.   Why, Mr. Maude, do you know
what happened that night when you met us
in the cold, outside the theatre at Aberdeen,
when the manager had told us he didn't want
us any more, and we knew that we had hardly
money enough when we had paid for our
lodging for that week to find us food for the
next ?'

There was colour enough in her face now,
as she clasped her hands together and leant
forward upon the table, with her blue eyes
glistening, her sensitive lips quivering slightly,
and a most sweet expression of affection and
gratitude illuminating her whole face.   I gave
her only an inarticulate, guttural murmur for
answer, and she went on with a thrill in her
voice.

'You spoke first, and mamma hurried on,

not knowing your voice, and of course I went
with her. But though I scarcely looked at
you, and certainly did not recognise you,
there was something in your manner, in the
sound of your voice, though I couldn't hear
what you said—something kind, something
chivalrous, that seemed to speak to one's
heart, and made me sorry she didn't stop.
And then, you know, you came after us, and
spoke again ; and I heard what you said that
time, and I whispered to mamma who you
were. And then, while you were talking to
her, and I only stood and listened, I felt
suddenly quite happy, for a minute before I
had wondered where the help was coming
from, and now I knew. And I was right
you see.' She bent her head, with an earnest
face, to emphasise her words. 'So that
when poor mamma used to warn me afterwards of the wickedness of men it all meant
nothing to me. For I only knew one man,

and he was everything that was good and noble, giving us shelter and sympathy and beautiful delicate kindness ; and to me time and thought and care that made me, out of a little ignorant girl, a thinking woman.   If that was not charity, what was it ? '

Now I could have told her what it was ; indeed with that little tender flower-face look- ing so ardently up into mine it did really need a strong effort not to tell her.   In the flow of her grateful recollections she had for- gotten that, the grandfatherly manner I had cultivated for so long perhaps aiding her ; but I think, as I kept silence, a flash of the truth came to her, for she grew suddenly shy, and instead of going on with the list of my bene- factions, as she had been evidently prepared to do, she took up the lace pocket-handker- chief which had been one of my gifts to Miss Farington, and became deeply interested in the pattern of the border.   After a pause she continued in a much more self - controlled manner.

'If Miss Farington's charity had been real, she would have been interested in the people you had been kind to.'

'Now you do the poor girl injustice. She took the greatest possible interest in you, for she was jealous.'

'Jealous! Oh no,' said Babiole with unexpected decision; and she caught her breath as she went on rapidly. 'One may hate the people one is jealous of, but one does not despise them. One may speak of them bitterly and scornfully, but all the time one is almost praying to them in one's heart to have mercy—to let go what they care for so little, what one cares for one's self so much. One's coldness to a person one is really jealous of is only a thin crust through which the fire peeps and flashes out. Miss Farington was not jealous!'

It was easy enough to see that poor Babiole spoke from experience of the passion ; and this conviction filled me with rage against her husband, and against myself for having brought about her marriage with such an unappreciative brute. It is always difficult to realise another person's neglect of a treasure you have found it hard to part with ; so I sat silently considering Fabian's phenomenal insensibility for some minutes until at last I asked abruptly—

'Who did he make you jealous of ?'

Babiole, who had also been deep in thought, started.

'Fabian ?' said she in a low voice. Then, trying to laugh, she added hastily, 'Oh, I was silly, I was jealous of everybody. You see I didn't know anything, and because I thought of nobody but him, I fancied he ought to think of nobody but me—which of course was unreasonable.'

'I don't think so,' said I curtly. 'Unless
I gave a woman all my affection I shouldn't
expect all hers.'

'Ah, *you!*' she exclaimed with a tender
smile. 'There was the mistake ; without
knowing it I had been forming my estimate
of men on what I felt to be true of you.' I
did not look at her ; but by the way in which
she hurried on after this ingenuous speech,
I knew that a sudden feeling of womanly
shame at her impulsive frankness had set
her blushing. 'But really Fabian was
quite reasonable,' she went on. 'He only
wanted me to give to him what he gave
to me — or at least he thought so,' she
corrected.

'And what was that ?'

'Well, just enough affection to make us
amiable towards each other when it was impossible to avoid a *tête-à-tête.*'

'But he can't have begun like that ! He

admired you, was fond of you. No man
begins by avoiding a bride like you!'

'Ah, that was the worst of it! For six
weeks he seemed to worship me, and I—I
never knew whether it was wet or fine—warm
or cold. Every wind blew from the south
for me, neither winter nor death could come
near the earth again. We were away, you
know, in Normandy and Brittany—when I
try to think of heaven I always see the sea
with the sun on it, and the long stretches of
sand. Before we came back I knew—I felt
—that a change was coming, that life would
not be always like that ; but I did not know, of
course I could not know, what a great change
it would be. Fabian said, " Our holiday is
over now, dearest, we must get to work again !
My Art is crying to me." Well, I was ready
enough to yield to the claims of Art, real Art,
not the poor ghost of it papa used to call
up ; and I was eager for my husband to take

a foremost place among artists, as I knew and
felt he could do.   But when we got back to
England—to London—to this Art which was
calling to us to shorten our holiday, I found
—or thought I found—that it had handsome
aquiline features, and a title, and that it wore
splendid gowns of materials which my husband
had to choose, and that it found its own husband and its own friends wearisome, and—
well, that Fabian was painting her portrait,
which was to make his fortune and proclaim
him a great painter.'

'Who was she?' I asked in a low voice.

She named the beautiful countess whose
portrait I had seen on Scott's mantelpiece
on the morning when I visited him at his
chambers.

'She came to our rooms several times for
sittings, as she had gone to his studio before
he married me.   But she found it was too far
to come—Bayswater being so much farther

than Jermyn Street from Kensington Palace
Gardens!—and he had to finish the picture
in her house. How the world swam round
me, and my brain hammered in my head on
those dreadful days when I knew he was with
her, glancing at her with those very glances
which used to set my heart on fire and make
me silent with deep passionate happiness. I
had seen him look at her like that when he
gave her those few sittings which she found
so tiresome because, I suppose, of my jealous
eyes. I never said anything—I didn't, indeed, Mr. Maude, for I knew he was the
man, and I was only the woman, and I must
be patient; but the misery and disappointment began to eat into my soul when I found
that those looks I had loved and cherished
so were never to be given to me again. At
first I thought it would be all right when this
portrait was painted and done with; this
brilliant lady's caprice of liking for my clever

husband would be over, and I should have, not only the careless kindness which never failed, but the old glowing warmth that I craved like a child starving in the snow. But it never came back.' A dull hopelessness was coming into her voice as she continued speaking, and her great eyes looked yearn-ingly out over the feathery larches in the avenue to the darkening sky. 'When that picture was finished there were other pictures, and there were amateur theatricals to be superintended, where the "eye of a true artist" was wanted, but where there was no use at all for a true artist's wife. And there were little scented notes to be answered, and their writers to be called upon ; and as I had from the first accepted Fabian's assurance that an artist's marriage could be nothing more than an episode in his life, and that the less it interrupted the former course of his life the happier that marriage would be, there was nothing for me but to submit, and to live on, as I told you, outside.'

'But you were wrong, you should have spoken out to him—reproached him, moved him!' I burst out—jumping up, and playing, in great excitement, with the things on the mantelpiece, unable to keep still.

'I did,' she answered sadly. 'One night, when he was going to the theatre to act as usual—he had just got an engagement—he told me not to sit up, he was going to the Countess's to meet some great foreign painter —I forget his name. The mention of her name drove me suddenly into a sort of frenzy; for he had just been sweet to me, and I had fancied—just for a moment, that the old times might come back. And I forgot all my caution, all my patience. I said angrily, "The Countess, the Countess! Am I never to hear the last of her? What do you want in this idle great lady's drawing-rooms when your own wife is wearing her heart out for you at home ?" Then his face changed, and I shook and trembled with terror. For he looked at me as if I had been some hateful creeping thing that had suddenly appeared before him in the midst of his enjoyment. He drew himself away from me, and said in a voice that seemed to cut through me, " I had no idea you were jealous." I faltered out, " No, no," but he interrupted me. " Please don't make a martyr of yourself, Babiole. Since you desire it, I shall come straight home from the theatre." '

' He ought to have married Miss Faring-ton !' said I heartily.

Babiole went on : ' I called to him not to do so; begged him not to mind my silly words. But he went out without speaking to me again. All the evening I tortured myself with reproaches, with fears, until, almost mad, I was on the point of going to the

theatre to implore him to forgive and forget
my wretched paltry jealousy. But I hoped
that he would not keep his word. I was
wrong. Before I even thought the piece
could be over he returned, having come as he
said, straight home. I don't think he can
know, even now, how horribly cruel he was
to me that night. He meant to give me a
lesson, but he did not know how thorough the
lesson would be. Seeing that he had come
back, although against his wish, I tried my
very utmost to please, to charm him, to show
him how happy his very presence could make
me. He answered me, he talked to me, he
told me interesting things—but all in the tone
he would have used to a stranger, placing a
barrier between us which all my efforts could
not move. In fact he showed me clearly
once for all that, however kind and courteous
he might be to me, I had no more influence
over him than one of the lay figures in his

studio. That night I could not sleep, but next morning I was a different woman. A little water will make a fire burn more fiercely; a little more puts it out. Even Fabian, though he did not really care for me, could not think the change in me altogether for the better; but his deliberate unkindness had suddenly cleared my sight and shown me that I was beating out my soul against a rock of hard immovable selfishness. He was nicer to me after a while, for he began to find out that he had lost something when I made acquaintances who thought me first interesting and presently amusing. But he never asked me for the devotion he had rejected, he never wanted it; he is always absorbed in half a dozen new passions; a Platonic friendship with a beauty, a furious dispute with an artist of a different school, a wild admiration for a rising talent. And so I have become, as I was bound to become, loving him as I did, just what he said an artist's wife should be—a slave; getting the worst, the least happy, the least worthy, part of his life, and all the time remaining discontented, and chafing against the chain.'

'Yet you have never had cause to be seriously jealous?'

Babiole hesitated, blushed, and the tears came to her eyes.

'I don't know. And—I know it sounds wicked, but I could almost say I don't care. I am to my husband like an ingenious automaton, moving almost any way its possessor pleases; but it has no soul—and I think he hardly misses that!'

'But that is nonsense, my dear child; you have just as much soul as ever.'

'Oh yes, it has come to life again here among the hills. But when I go back to London——'

'Well?'

' I shall leave it up here—with you—to take care of till I come back again.'

She had risen and was half laughing; but there was a tremor in her voice.

' Where are you going?' I asked as I saw her moving towards the door.

' I am going to see if there is a letter from Fabian to say when he is coming. I saw Tim come up the avenue with the papers.'

' But Fabian can't know himself yet!' I objected. However that might be, she was gone, leaving me to a consideration of the brilliant ability I had shown in match-making, both for myself and my friends.

CHAPTER XXIV

WHEN I joined Mrs. Ellmer and her daughter
that evening, I found that the former lady
was oppressed by the conviction that 'something had happened,' something interesting
of which there was an evil design abroad to
keep her in ignorance. She had been
questioning Babiole I felt sure, and getting
no satisfactory replies; for while there was
a suspicious halo of pale rose-colour—which
in my sight did not detract from her beauty
—about the younger lady's eyes, her mother
made various touching references to the
cruelty of want of confidence, and at last,
after several tentative efforts, got on the

right track by observing that my 'young
lady' was not very exacting, since I had not
been near her that day.   This remark set
both her daughter and me blushing furiously,
and Mrs. Ellmer, figuratively speaking, gave
the 'view halloo.'   After a very short run I
was brought to earth, and confessed that—er
—Miss Farington and I—er—had had a—in
fact a disagreement—a mere lover's quarrel.
It would soon blow over—but just at present
—that is for a day or two, why——

Mrs. Ellmer interrupted my laboured
explanation with a delighted and shrill little
giggle.

'And so you've had a quarrel! Well,
really, Mr. Maude, as an old friend, you
must allow me to take this opportunity—
before you make it up again, you know—to
tell you that really I think you are throwing
yourself away.'

The truth was that the poor little woman

had been smarting, ever since Miss Farington's visit, from the supercilious scorn with
which that well-informed young lady had
treated her.   I protested, but very mildly ;
for, indeed, to hear a little gentle disapproba-
tion of my late too matter-of-fact love gave
me no acute pain.

'I wouldn't for the world have said anything before, you know, for if, of course, a
person's love affairs are not his own business, whose are they ?   But having known
you so long, I really must say, now that
I can open my lips without indiscretion, that
the moment I saw that stuck-up piece of
affectation I said to myself: "She must
have asked him!"'

I assured Mrs. Ellmer that was not the
case, but she paid little heed to my contra-
diction.   She had relieved her feelings, that
was the great thing, and it was with recovered
calmness that she inquired after the friends

who had made my yearly shooting party in
the old times. I knew little more of them
than she did; for that last gathering, when
Fabian won my pretty witch's heart, had
indeed been the farewell meeting predicted
by Maurice Brown. That young author
having shocked the public with one exceedingly nasty novel, had followed it up by
another which would have shocked them still
more if they had read it; this, however, they
refrained from doing with a unanimity which
might have proved disastrous to his reputation if a well-known evening paper had not
offered him a good berth as a sort of inspec-
tor of moral nuisances, a post which the
clever young Irishman filled with all the
requisite zeal and indiscretion. As for Mr.
Fussell, he had done well for himself in the
city, and now leased a shooting-box of his
own. While Edgar, my dear old friend and
chum, had fallen back into the prosperous

ranks of the happily married, and was now less troubled by political ambition than by a tendency to grow fat.

The ten days which followed the rupture of my engagement to Miss Farington passed in a great calm, troubled only by a growing sense of dread, both to Babiole and me, of what was to come after.   She got well rapidly, quite well, as nervous emotional creatures do when once the moral atmosphere about them is right.   For it was the loving sympathy of every living being round her, from her mother down—or up to Ta-ta, which worked the better part of her cure, though I admit that the hills and the fir-trees and the fresh sweet air had their share in it.   She went out every day, sometimes with her mother and me, oftener with me and Ta-ta, as Mrs. Ellmer's strong dislike to walking exercise did not decrease as the years rolled on.   As for Babiole, I thank

God that the pleasure of those walks in the crisp air up the hills and through the glens was unallayed for her. The tarnish which want of warmth and sympathy had breathed on her childlike and trusting nature was wearing off; and her old faith in the companion to whom she had graciously given a place in her heart as the incarnation of kindness had only grown the stronger for the glimpses she had lately had of something deeper underneath. I even think that in the languid and irresponsible convalescence of her heart and mind from the wounds her unlucky marriage had dealt to both, she cherished a superstitious feeling that now I had returned from my travels it would come all right, and that I should be able to mend the defects of the marriage by another exercise of the magical skill which had brought it about. So she chattered or sang or was silent at her pleasure, as we walked between

the now bare hedges beside the swollen Dee,
or climbed on a thick carpet of rustling
brown oak leaves up Craigendarroch, and
noticed how day by day the mantle of snow
on Lochnagar grew wider and ampler, and
how the soft wail of the wind among the fir-
trees in summer-time had grown into an
angry and threatening roar, as if already
hungering for those days and nights of loud
March when the tempest would tear up the
young saplings from the mountain-sides like
reeds and hurl them down pell-mell over the
decaying trunks which already choked up
the hill-paths, and told of the storms of past
years. She would look into my face from
time to time to see if I was happy, for she
had got the trick of reading through that
ugly mask; if the look satisfied her, she
either talked or was silent as she pleased, but
if she fancied she detected the least sign of
a cloud, she never rested until, by sweet

words and winning looks, she had driven it away.

I, poor devil, was of course happy after a very different fashion. The blood has not yet cooled to any great extent at six and thirty, and blue eyes that have haunted you for seven years lose none of their witchery at that age, when the demon Reason throws his weight into the scale on the side of Evil, and tells you that the years are flitting by, carrying away the time for happiness, and that the beauty which steeps you to the soul in longing has been left unheeded by its possessor like a withered flower. But Babiole's perfect confidence was her safe-guard and mine, and like the wind among the pines, I kept my tumults within due bounds. I was, however, occasionally dis-tressed by a consideration for which I had never cared a straw before—what the neigh-bours would say. If I, an indifferent honest

man, really had some trouble in keeping unworthy thoughts and impulses down within
me, what sort of conduct these carrion-hunt-
ing idiots would ascribe to a man, whom
they looked upon as an importer of foreign
vices and the type of all that was godless
and lawless, was pretty evident. They
would all, in a commonplace chorus, take the
part of the commonplace Miss Farington,
and unite in condemnation of poor Babiole.
Now no man likes to let the reputation of
his queen of the earth be pulled to pieces by
a cackling crew of idiots, and, therefore,
though I had not enough strength of mind to
suggest giving up those treasured walks, I
began, torn by my struggling feelings, to
look forward feverishly to the letter which
Fabian had promised to send off as soon as
he knew on what date he would be free to
come north. His wife herself showed no
eagerness.

'He is the very worst of correspondents,'
she said.   'He will probably write a letter
to say he is coming just before starting, post
it at one of the last stations he passes
through, and arrive here before it.'

It did not comfort me to learn thus that
he might come at any moment.   My conscience was pretty clear, but I wanted to
have a fair notice of his arrival, that I might
receive him in such a manner as to prepare
the peccant husband for the desperately
earnest sermon I had made up my mind to
preach him on what his wife called neglect,
but what I felt sure was infidelity.

A very serious addition to the cares I felt
on behalf of my old pupil came upon me in
the shape of a rumour, communicated by Ferguson in a mysterious manner, that a strange
figure had been seen by the keepers in the
course of the past week, wandering about the
hills in the daytime and hovering in the

vicinity of the Hall towards evening. I
spoke with one of the men who had seen
him, and from what he said I could have no
doubt that the wanderer was the unlucky
Ellmer who, as I found by sending off a
telegram to the lunatic asylum where he had
been for some time confined, had been missing for four days and was supposed to be
dangerous. I at once gave orders for a
search to be made for him, being much
alarmed by the possibility of his presenting
himself suddenly to either of the two poor
ladies, who were not even aware of his condition. The first day's scouring of the hills
and of the forest proved fruitless, however,
while Babiole was much surprised at the pertinacity with which I insisted that the wind
was too keen for her to go out. On the
second day I think she began to have sus-
picions that something was being kept from
her, for on my suggesting that she had better

stay indoors again, as the keepers were out shooting very near the Hall, she gave me a shy apprehensive glance, but made no remonstrance. As I started to 'make a round with the keeper,' as I truly told her, though I did not explain with what object, she came to the door with me, making a beautiful picture under the ivy of the portico, her white throat rising out of her dark gown like a lily, and the pink colour which the mountain air had brought back again flushing and fading in her face.

'Well,' said I, looking at her with a great yearning over the fairness and brightness which were so soon to disappear from my sight, to be swallowed up in the fogs and the fever of London life, 'Well, I shall call at the post-office, and see if I can't charm out of the post-mistress's fingers a letter from Fabian.'

'Ah, you want to get rid of us!' said she, half smiling, half reproachful.

' No-o,' said I, looking down at my gaiters, ' Not so particularly.'

Then we neither of us said any more, but stood without looking at each other. I don't know what she was thinking about, but I know that I began to grow blind and deaf even to the sight of her and the sound of the tapping of her little foot upon the step ; the roar of the rain-swollen Muick in the valley below seemed to have come suddenly nearer, louder, to be thundering close to my ears, raising to tempest height the passionate excitement within me, and shrieking out forebodings of the desolation which would fall upon me when my poor witch should have fled away. I was thankful to be brought back to commonplace by the shrill tones of Mrs. Ellmer, who had followed her daughter to the doorstep, and who encouraged me with much banter about my shooting powers as I set off.·

The gillie who accompanied me was a long, lank, weedy young Highlander, silent and shrewd, who was already a valuable servant, and who promised to develop into a fine specimen of stalwart Gaelic humanity before many years were over. We made the circuit of that part of the forest near the Hall which had been appointed our beat for the day, but failed to find any trace of the fugitive. Jock was not surprised at this.

'A mon wi' a bee in's bonnet's nae sa daft but a' can mak' the canny ones look saft if a' will,' said he with a wise look.

And his opinion, which I apprehensively shared, was that the fugitive would not be secured until he had given us some trouble.

It was a cold and gloomy day. The chilling penetrating Scotch mist shrouded the whole landscape with a mournful gray veil, and gave place, as the day wore on and the leaden clouds grew heavier, to a thin but

steady snow-fall.   I left Jock, as the time
drew near for the arrival of the train that
brought the London letters, to return to the
Hall without me, and got to Ballater post-
office just as the mail-bag was being carried
across from the little station, which is just
opposite.   In a few minutes I had got my
papers, and a letter for Babiole in her husband's handwriting.   The snow was falling
faster by this time, and already drifting
before the rising wind into little heaps and
ridges by the wayside and on the exposed
stretch of somewhat bare and barren land
which lies between Ballater and the winding
Dee.   I walked back at a quick pace, scan-
ning the small snow-drifts narrowly, measur-
ing with my eyes the progress the soft white
covering was making, and wondering with
the foolish heart-quiver and miracle-hunger
of a school-boy on the last day of the
holidays, whether that snow-fall would have

the courage and strength of mind to go on bravely as it had begun, and snow us up! If only the train would stop running—it did sometimes in the depths of a severe winter—and cut off all possibility of my witch being taken away from me for another month. I had worshipped her so loyally, I had been so 'good,' as she used to say—I couldn't resist giving myself this little pat on the back—that surely Providence might trust me with my wistful but well-conducted happiness a little longer. And all the time I knew that my solicitous questionings of sky and snow were futile and foolish, that I was carrying the death-warrant of my dangerous felicity in my pocket, and that if I had a spark of sense or manliness left in my wool-gathering old head, I ought to be heartily glad of it.

The notion of the death-warrant disturbed me, however, and when I burst into the drawing room where Mrs. Ellmer was darning a handsome old tapestry curtain, and looking, with her worn delicate face, pink with interest, rather pretty over it, I felt nervous as I asked for Babiole. She entered behind me before the question was out of my mouth, and I put the letter into her hands without another word, and retreated to one of the windows while she opened and read it. She was moved too, and her little fingers shook as they tore the envelope. I felt so guiltily anxious to know whether she was pleased that I was afraid if I glanced in her direction she would look up suddenly and detect my meanness. So I looked out of the window and watched the snow collecting on the branches of the firs outside, while Mrs. Ellmer, without pausing in her work, wondered volubly whether Fabian wasn't ashamed of himself for having left his wife so long without a letter, and would like to know what he had got to say for himself now he had written. Then sud-

denly the mother gave a little piercing cry,
and I, turning at once, saw that Babiole,
standing on the same spot where I had seen
her last, and holding her husband's letter
tightly clenched in her hands, seemed to have
changed in a moment from a young, sweet,
and beautiful woman into a livid and haggard
old one.   She had lost all command of the
muscles of her face, and while her eyes, from
which the dewy blue had faded, stared out
before her in a meaningless gaze, the pallid
lips of her open mouth twitched convulsively,
although she did not attempt to utter a
word.

Her mother was by her side in a moment,
while I stood looking stupidly on, articulating
hoarsely and with difficulty—

'The letter!   Is it the letter!'

Mrs. Ellmer snatched the paper out of her
daughter's hands so violently that she tore it,
and supporting Babiole with one arm, read

the letter through to the end, while I kept my eyes fixed upon her in a tumult of feelings I did not dare to analyse. As she read the last word she tossed it over to me with her light eyes flashing like steel.

'Read it, read it!' she cried, as the paper fell at my feet. 'See what sort of a husband you have given my poor child!'

The words and the action roused Babiole, who had scarcely moved except to shiver in her mother's arms. She drew herself away as if stung back to life, and a painful rush of blood flowed to her face and neck as she made two staggering steps forward, picked up the letter, and walked quietly, noiselessly, with her head bent and her whole frame drooping with shame, out of the room. Mrs. Ellmer would have followed, but I stopped her.

'Don't go,' I said in a husky voice. 'Leave her to herself a little while first. If she wants comforting, it will come with more

force later when she has got over the first
shock.   What was it ?'

'Oh, nothing,' said Mrs. Ellmer, who had
become more acid on her daughter's behalf
than she had ever been on her own.   'Nothing
but what every married woman must expect.'

'Well, and what's that ?'

She gave a little grating laugh.

'You a man and you ask that!'

'I'm a man, but not a married man, remember.   Don't impute to me the mis-
demeanours I have had no chance of com-
mitting.   Now what was it?   Fabian wrote
unkindly, I suppose.'

'Oh, *dear* no.   It was very much the
kindest letter from him I have ever seen.'

'Did he put off his coming then ?'

'Not at all.   He made an appointment to
meet his darling in Edinburgh.'

'Edinburgh!'   I echoed in amazement.
'Why Edinburgh ?'

'Why not, Mr. Maude?' said she, in a harder voice than ever. 'It's a very pretty place, and two people who are fond of each other may spend a pleasant enough time together there. Only Mr. Scott spoilt his nice little plan by a stupid mistake. Into the envelope he had addressed to his wife he slipped his letter to another woman!'

With a glance of disgust at me which was meant to include my whole sex, Mrs. Ellmer, with the best tragic manner of her old stage days, left me stupefied with rage and remorse, as she sailed out of the room.

CHAPTER XXV

At the time when the mind is oppressed by a long-gathering cloud of passionate yet scarcely defined anxiety, the awakening crash of an event, even of an event tragic in its consequences, is a relief. This miserable letter, therefore, exposing as it did in unmistakable terms Fabian's infidelity, shook me free of the morbid imaginings and unwholesome yearnings to which I had lately been a prey, and set me the more worthy task of devising some means of helping both my friends out of the deadlock to which I myself had unwittingly helped them to come.

For the first time I was sorry for Fabian. A serious fault committed by a person whom accidents of birth or circumstance have brought near to one's self sets one thinking of one's own 'near shaves,' and after that the tide of mercy flows in steadily. How was I, who had never been able to conquer my own love for an unattainable woman, to blame this man of much more combustible temperament, whom I had myself induced to form a marriage with a girl whom I had no means of knowing to be first in his heart? I would take no high moral tone with him now; I would speak to him frankly as man to man, hold myself blameworthy for my own share in the unlucky matrimonial venture, and appeal to the sense and kindness I knew he possessed not to let the punishment for my indiscretion fall upon the only one of us three who was entirely free from blame. There crossed my mind at this point of my reflections an unpleasant remembrance of the manner in which Fabian had received a somewhat similar appeal from me years ago, and down at the bottom of my heart there lurked a conviction that he would hear whatever I might say without offence, and neglect it without scruple. However, it was impossible to be silent now; and as the gray day dissolved into darkness, and the only light in the study, to which I had retreated, came from the glowing peat-fire, I got up from the old leather chair which was consecrated to my reveries, and with one glance through the eastern window out at the great woolly flakes of snow that were now falling thickly, I left the room and went in search of Mrs. Ellmer.

I heard her voice in her daughter's room, and knocking at the door, called to her softly. She came out at once, and by her gentle manner I judged that she was already contrite for having treated me so cavalierly at our late interview.

'How is Babiole?' I asked first.

'She is quiet now and much better, Mr. Maude. Would you like to see her?'

'Well, no; I couldn't do her so much good as you can. I wanted to speak to you. I've been thinking; of course Fabian wrote two letters, and put them into the wrong envelopes. Then the letter he intended for his wife told her when he was coming, while the other letter made an appointment on the way. Can you find out by the letter which has come to your hands when he expects to arrive here?'

'It was written the night before last; the appointment was for last night,' answered she with a fresh access of acidity.

'Then he probably meant to come on here to-day. I think I'll go to Ballater and meet the six o'clock train; I shall just have time.

And if he doesn't come by that I'll telegraph
to Edinburgh.   What address does he give
there ?'

'Royal Hotel.   But you don't suppose
that he will dare to come on here when he
finds out what he has done ?'

'I don't suppose he will find out till he
gets here.'

'I hope, Mr. Maude, if he does come, you
will persuade Babiole to show a little spirit.
She seems inclined at present to receive him
back like a lamb.'

I was sorry to hear this, because it suggested to me that her feeling for her huband
had declined even below the point of indifference.   I left Mrs. Ellmer and went downstairs to put on my mackintosh and prepare
for my tramp in the snow.   The lamp in the
hall had not yet been lighted, and I was fumbling in the darkness for my deer-stalker on
the pegs of the hat-stand when I heard my

name called in a hoarse whisper from the staircase just above me. I turned, and saw the outline of Babiole's head against the faint candle-light which fell upon the landing above through the open door of her room.

'Mr. Maude,' she repeated, trying to clear and steady her voice. 'Where are you going?'

'Only as far as the village,' said I in a robust and matter-of-fact tone.

'Are you going to meet Fabian?'

'Yes, if he is anywhere about.'

'Ah, I thought so!' burst from her lips in a sharp whisper. She came down two more steps hurriedly: 'You are not to reproach him, Mr. Maude, you are not to plead for me, do you hear? What good can you do by interceding for a love which is dead? I was jealous when I read that letter, but not so jealous as shocked, wounded. And now that I have thought a little I am not jealous

at all; so what right have I to be even
wounded ? This lady he wrote to he has
admired for a long time, and though I never
knew anything before, I guessed. She is a
beauty, her photograph is in all the windows,
and a little fringe of scandal hangs about her.
She has dash, *éclat*, brilliancy ; I have heard
him say so. So he is consistent, you see,
after all. I can acknowledge that now, and
I don't feel angry.'

Her voice was indeed quite calm, although
unutterably sad. But I noticed and rejoiced
in the absence of that bitterness which had
jarred on me so painfully in London.

' I do though,' I said gruffly.

' But you must not show it. You cannot
reconcile us through the heart, for you cannot
make him a different man. You must be
satisfied with knowing that you have made
me a better wife. I am just as much stronger
in heart and mind as I am in health since I

have been up here ; I wanted to tell you that while I had the opportunity, to tell you that you have cured me, and to—thank you.'

As she uttered the last words in a low, sweet, lingering tone, a light burst suddenly upon us and showed me what the darkness had hidden—an expression on her pale face of beautiful strength and peace, as if indeed the quiet hills and the dark sweet-scented forests and the two human hearts that cared for her had poured some elixir into her soul to fortify it against indifference and neglect.

A little dazzled and befooled by her lovely appearance, I stood gazing at her face without a thought as to where the idealising light came from, until I heard at the other end of the hall a grating preliminary cough, and turning, saw that it was Ferguson, entering with the lamp, who had brought about this poetical effect. He had something to say to me evidently, since instead of advanc-

ing to place the light on its usual table, he
remained standing at a distance still and stiff
as a statue of resignation, as his custom was
when his soul was burning to deliver itself
of an unsolicited communication.

'Well, Ferguson!' said I.

'Yes, sir,' said he, with another cough.

But he did not come forward. Now I
knew this was a sign that he considered
his errand serious, and I moved a few steps
towards him and beckoned him to me.

'Anything to tell me?' I asked; and as he
glanced at Babiole I came nearer still.

'Jock has just been in to say, sir, that a
gun has been stolen from his cottage.'

Babiole, who had not moved away, overheard, and must have guessed the import of
this, for I heard behind me a long-drawn
breath caused by some sudden emotion.

'When did he miss it?' I asked in a very
low voice.

'Just now, sir. He came straight here
to tell you of it. It must have been taken
while he was out on his rounds this afternoon.'

I did not think the poor crack-brained
creature whom I guessed to be the thief was
likely to do much mischief with his prize.
But I told Ferguson to put all the keepers on
their guard, and to take care that such crazy
old bolts and bars as we used in that primi-
tive part of the world should be drawn and
raised, so that the unlucky fugitive should
not be able to possess himself of any more
weapons. I also directed that the search
about the grounds should be kept up, and
that if the poor wretch were caught, he was
to be treated with all gentleness, and taken
to the now disused cottage to await my
return.

It was now so late that if Fabian had
come by the four o'clock train he must by

this time be half way from the station. But it was possible that he had already discovered the mistake of the letters, and had felt a shyness about continuing a journey which was likely to bring him to a cold welcome ; so I stuck to my intention of going to Ballater either to meet him if he had arrived, or to telegraph to him if he had not. When I had finished speaking to Ferguson, I found that Babiole had disappeared from the hall. I was rather glad of it ; for I had dreaded her questioning, and I hurried the preparations for my walk so that in a few moments I was out of the house and safe from the difficult task of calming her fears.

It was already night when I shut the hall-door behind me and stepped out on to the soft white covering which was already thick on the ground. The snow was still falling thickly, and the only sound I heard, as I groped my way under the arching trees of

the avenue, was the occasional swishing noise
of a load of snow that, dislodged by a fresh
burden from the upper branch of a fir-tree,
brushed the lower boughs as it fell to the earth.
I am constitutionally untroubled by nervous
tremors, and I was too deeply occupied with
thoughts of Fabian and his wife to give much
grave consideration to possible danger from
the unhappy lunatic who was now in all probability hidden somewhere in the neighbourhood with a weapon in his possession ; but
when in the oppressive darkness and stillness
the tramp of footsteps in the soft snow just
behind me fell suddenly on my ears, I
confess that it was with my heart in my
mouth, as the dairymaids say, that I turned
and raised threateningly the thick stick I
carried. It was, however, only Jock, gun
in hand as usual, who had run fast to overtake me, and had come upon me sooner than
he expected, the small lantern he carried

in his hand being of little use in the darkness.

'What made you come, Jock?' I asked,
not, to tell the truth, sorry to have a companion upon the lonely forest road which
seemed on this night, for obvious reasons, a
more gloomy promenade than usual.

'Mistress Scott bid me gang wi' ye, sir,'
answered he. 'She said the necht was sae
dark ye might miss the pairth by the
burn.'

We walked on together in silence until,
having left the avenue far behind us, we
were well in the hilly and winding road
which runs through the forest from Loch
Muick to the Dee. At one of the many
bends in the roadway Jock suddenly stopped
and stood in a listening attitude.

'Deer?' said I.

'Nae,' answered he, after a pause, in a
measured voice, 'It's nae deer.'

He said no more, but examined the barrels of his gun by the light of the lantern, and walked on at a quicker pace. I had heard nothing, but his manner put me on the alert, and it was with a sense of coming adventure that, peering before me in the darkness and straining my ears to catch the faintest sound, I strode on beside the sturdy young Highlander. Warned as I was, it was with a sickening horror that, a moment later, I too heard sounds which had already caught his keener ears. Muffled by the falling snow, by the intervening trees, there came faintly through the air the hoarse yelping cries of a madman. I glanced at the stolid figure by my side.

'Was that what you heard, Jock?' I asked stupidly, more anxious for the sound of his voice than for his answer.

'I dinna ken, sir, if ye heard what I heard,' said he cautiously.

All the while we were walking at our best
pace through the snow.   It seemed a long
time before, at one of the sharpest turns of
the road, Jock laid his hand on my shoulder
and we stopped.   There was nothing to be
seen but trees, trees, the patch of clear snow
before us and the falling flakes.   But we
could plainly hear the noise of tramping feet
and hoarse guttural cries—

'I've done it, I've done it!   I said I
would, and I've kept my word!   I've done
it, I've done it, I've done it!'

The tramping feet seemed to beat time
to the words.   I had hardly distinguished
these cries when I started forward again, and
dashing round the angle of the road with a
vague fear at my heart, I came close upon
the wild weird figure of the unhappy madman who, with his hat off and his long lank
hair tossed and dishevelled, was dancing un-
couthly in the deep shadow of the trees and

chanting to himself the words we had heard.
On the ground at one side of him lay the
stolen gun, and at the other, close to the
bank which bordered the road on the left,
was some larger object, which in the profound
darkness I could not at first define. With a
sudden spring I easily seized the lunatic and
held him fast, while Jock lifted the lantern
high so as to see his face. As the rays of
light fell upon me, however, Mr. Ellmer,
who had been too utterly bewildered by the
sudden attack to make sign or sound, gave
forth a loud cry, and staring at me with
starting eyeballs and distorted shaking lips
stammered out—

'It's he, he himself! Come back! Oh
my God, I am cursed, cursed!'

In the surprise and fear these words inspired me with I released my hold, so that he
might with a very slight effort have shaken
himself free of my grasp. But he stood

quite still, as if overmastered by some power
that he did not dare to dispute, and allowed
himself to be transferred from my keeping
to Jock's without any show of resistance.
As soon as my hands were thus free, the
young Highlander silently passed me the
lantern, which I took in a frenzy of excitement which precluded the reception of any
defined dread. I fell back a few steps until
the faint rays of the light I carried showed
me, blurred by the falling snow, the outline
of the dark object I had already seen on the
white ground. It was the body of a man. I
had known that before ; I knew no more now ;
but an overpowering sickness and dizziness
came upon me as I glanced down, blotting out
the sight from before my eyes, and filling me
with the cowardly craving we have all of us
known to escape from an existence which
has brought a sensation too deadly to be
borne. Every mad impulse of the passion

with which I had lately been struggling, every vague wish, every feeling of jealous resentment seemed to spring to life again in my heart, and turn to bitter gnawing remorse. I think I must have staggered as I stood, for I felt my foot touch something, and at the shock my sight came to me again and I knelt down in the snow.

'Fabian, Fabian, old fellow!' I called in a husky voice.

He was lying on his face. I put my arm under him and turned him over and wiped the snow from his lips and forehead. His eyes were wide open, but they did not see me; they had looked their last on the world and on men. The blood was still flowing from a bullet wound just under the left ribs, and his body was not yet cold.

Mad Mr. Ellmer, in the snow and the darkness, had mistaken Fabian for me. He had sworn he would kill the man who should destroy his daughter's happiness, and fate or fortune or the providence which has strange freaks of justice had blinded his poor crazy eyes and enabled him most tragically to keep his word.

CHAPTER XXVI

I STAYED beside the body of my dead friend while Jock, by my direction, returned to the Hall with the unhappy Ellmer, who had already fallen into a state of maudlin apathy, and was crying, not from remorse, but from the effects of cold, hunger, and exposure on his now wasted frame. He allowed himself to be led away like a child, and seemed cheered and soothed by the promise of food and fire. I wondered, as I watched him stagger along by the side of the stalwart Highlander, that the spirit of a not ignoble revenge should have kept its vitality so long in his breast in spite of enfeebled reason, poverty and degradation.

It was a terrible vigil that I was keeping. I knew by my own feelings that the shock of this tragic return to her would be a hundred times more severe to Babiole than if her bosom had been palpitating with sweet expectancy for the clasp of a loving husband's arms. Instead of the passionate yearning sorrow of a woman truly widowed, she would feel the far crueller stings of remorse none the less bitter that her conduct towards him had been blameless.

As for me, I remembered nothing but his brilliancy, his vivacity, the twinkling humour in his piercing eyes as he would stride up and down the room, pouring out upon any inoffensive person or thing that failed in the slightest respect to meet with his approval such vials of wrath as the less excitable part of mankind would reserve for abandoned scoundrels and nameless iniquities. With all his faults, there was a charm, an exuberant

warmth about Fabian that left a bare place in
the heart of his friends when he was gone.
As I leant over his dead body and gazed at
the still white face by the light of the lantern,
I wished from the depths of my heart that
Ellmer had shot down the man he hated, and
had left this poor lad to enjoy a few years
longer the beautiful world he loved with such
passionate ardour.

The snow-fall began to slacken as I waited
beside him, and when Jock returned from
the stable with Tim and another man, the
rising moon was struggling out from behind
the clouds, and giving promise of a fair night
after the bitter and stormy day. We laid
my dead friend on a hurdle and carried him
home to the Hall, while old Ta-ta, who had
come with the men, sniffed curiously at our
heels, and, divining something strange and
woeful in our dark and silent burden, followed
with her sleek head bent to the glistening

snow, and only offered one wistful wag of
her tail to assure me that if I were sad, well,
I knew she was so too.

I learnt from Jock that Mrs. Ellmer had
met her husband, and that, after the manner
of women, she had led him in and minis-
tered to his bodily wants while taking advantage of his weak and abject state to inflict
upon him such chastisement with her voluble
tongue as might well reconcile him to another
long absence from her. But Jock thought
that the poor wretch's wanderings were nearly
over.

'I doot if a's een will see the mornin' licht
again,' said the gillie gravely. 'A' speaks i'
whispers, an' shivers an' cries like a bairn. A'
must be verra bad, for a' doesna' mind the
lady's talk.'

'And Mrs. Scott, does she know?'

Jock looked solemn and nodded.

'Meester Ferguson told her, and he says

the poor leddy's crazed like, an' winna speak
nor move.'

I asked no more, and I remember no
further detail of that ghastly procession.   I
saw nothing but Babiole's face, her eyes looking straight into mine full of involuntary reproach to me for having unwittingly brought
yet another disaster upon her.

Ferguson met us at the door of the Hall,
and told me, in a voice which real distress
made only more harsh and guttural, that Mrs.
Ellmer had had the cottage unlocked, and
had caused fires to be lighted there for the
reception of her husband, the poor lady believing that he would give less trouble there.

'How is Mrs. Scott?' I asked anxiously.

Ferguson answered in a grating broken
whisper.

'She went away—by herself, sir—when I
told her—let her guess like—the thing that
had happened.'

They were taking Fabian's body to the little room where he used to sleep during our yearly meetings. As the slow tramp, tramp up the stairs began, I opened the door of my study, and entered with the subdued tread we instinctively affect in the neighbourhood of those whom no sound will ever disturb again. The lamp was on the table, but had not yet been turned up. The weak rays of the moon came through the south window; for the curtains were always left undrawn until I chose myself to close out the night-landscape. The fire was red and without flame. I advanced as far as the hearth-rug and stopped with a great shock. On the ground at my feet, her head resting face downward on the worn seat of my old leather chair, her hands pressed tightly to her ears, and her body drawn up as if in great pain, was Babiole; even as I watched her I saw that a shudder convulsed her from head to

foot, and left her as still as the dead.   Every
curve of her slight frame, the rigidity of her
arms, the evident discomfort of her cramped
attitude, told me that my poor child was a
prey to grief so keen that the dread of her
turning her face to meet mine made a coward
of me, and I took a hasty step backwards,
intending to retreat.   But the sight of her
had unmanned me ; my eyes were dim and I
'lost command of my steps.   I touched the
screen in my clumsy attempt to escape, and
To-to, disturbed from sleep, sprang up rattling
his chain and chattering loudly.

Babiole, with a low startled cry that was
scarcely more than a long-drawn breath,
changed her attitude, and her eyes fell upon
me.   I stood still, not knowing for the first
moment whether it would frighten her least
for me to disappear unseen or let her see that
it was only I.   But no sooner had she caught
sight of me than she turned and started up

upon her knees with a look on her face so
wild, so unearthly in its exaltation that my
heart seemed to stand still, and my very blood
to freeze with the fear that the mind of the
little lady had been unable to stand the shock
of her husband's death.

'Babiole, Babiole,' I said hoarsely; and
moved out of myself by my terrible fear, I
came back to her and stooped, and would
have raised her in my arms with the tenderness one feels for a helpless child alone in
the world, to try to soothe and comfort her.
But before my hands could touch her a great
change had passed over her, a change so
great, so marked, that there was no mistaking
its meaning; and breaking into a flood of
passionate tears, while her face melted from
its stony rigidity to infinite love and tenderness, she clasped her hands and whispered
brokenly, feverishly, but with the ardour of
an almost delirious joy—

'Thank God! Thank God! Then it was not you! They told me it was you!'

I stepped back, startled, speechless, overwhelmed by a rush of feelings that in my highly-wrought mood threw me into a kind of frenzy. Drunk with the transformation of my despair into full - fledged hope, and no longer master of myself, I stretched out a madman's arms to her, I heard my own voice uttering words wild, incoherent, without sense or meaning, that seemed to be forced out of my breast in spite of myself, under pressure of the frantic passion that had burst its bonds at the first unguarded moment, and spoilt at one blow all my hard-won record of self-control and self-restraint. She had sprung to her feet and evaded my touch; but as she stood at a little distance from me, her face still shone with the same radiance, and she looked, to my excited fancy, the very spirit of tender, impassioned, exalted human love, too sweet not to allure, too pure not to command respect. There was no fear in her expression, only a shade of grave gentle reproach. As she fixed her solemn eyes upon me I stammered and grew ashamed, and my arms dropped to my sides as the recollection of the tragedy which had brought us here came like a pall over my excited spirits. Then she came round the table on her way towards the door, and would have gone out without a word, I think, if the abject shame and self-disgust with which I hung my head and slunk out of her way had not moved her to pity. I was afraid she would not like to pass me, savage beast as I had shown myself to be, so I had turned my back to the door and moved towards my old chair. But Babiole was too noble-hearted to need any affectations of prudery, and to see her old friend humiliated was too painful for her to bear.

'Mr. Maude,' she called to me in a low voice, and the very sound of her voice brought healing to my wounded self-esteem.

I turned slowly, without lifting my eyes, and she held out her little hand for me to take.

'I am a great rough brute,' I said hoarsely. 'It is very good of you to forgive me.'

'You are our best friend, now and always,' she said, holding her hand steadily in mine. She continued with an effort : 'You are not hurt; then it is——'

She looked at me with eyes full of awe, but she was prepared for my answer.

'Fabian,' I whispered huskily.

'He is dead ?'   I scarcely heard the words as her white lips formed them.

'Yes.'

'God forgive me !' she said brokenly, while her eyes grew dark and soft with sorrow and shame ; then drawing her hand from mine, she crept with noiseless feet out of the room.

I remained in the study for some time, a prey to the most violent excitement, in which the emotions of grief and remorse struggled vainly against the intoxicating belief that Babiole loved me. I strode up and down what little space there was in the room, until the four walls could contain me no longer. Then for an hour I wandered about the forest, climbed up to the top of a rock which over-looked the Dee and the Braemar road, and came back in the moonlight by the shell of old Knock Castle, from which, three hundred years ago, James Gordon went forth to fight for his kinsman and neighbour, the Baron of Braickley, and fell by his side in one of the fierce and purposeless skirmishes which seem to have been the only occupation worth mentioning of the Highland gentlemen of those times. When I returned home I saw

Babiole's shadow through the blind of the little room where her husband's body was lying. It was long past my dinner hour, and I was so brutishly hungry that I felt thankful that neither of the unhappy ladies was present to be disgusted with my mountain appetite. I had scarcely risen from table when Ferguson informed me that Mrs. Ellmer had sent Tim to beg me to come to the cottage to see her husband, who she feared was dying. Remembering the poor wretch's ghastly and haggard appearance when we found him, I was not surprised ; nor could I, knowing the fate that might be in store for him if he lived, be sorry that his miserable life would in all probability end peacefully now.

I found him lying in bed in one of the upper rooms of the cottage with his wife standing by his side. His eyes were feverishly bright, and the hand he let me take felt dry and withered. He said nothing when I

asked him how he was, but stared at me intently while his wife spoke.

'He wanted to see you, Mr. Maude, just
while he felt a little better and able to speak,'
said she, 'to tell you how sorry he is for the
foolish and dreadful thoughts he had about
you, when he did not know the true state of
the case, and when his head was rather dizzy
because he had lived somewhat carelessly, you
know.'

Poor little woman! it was to her all my
sympathy went, to this brave, energetic, fragile creature whose worst faults were on the
surface, and who, to this bitter shameful end,
valiantly worked with her busy skilful hands,
and made the best of everything. She looked
so worn that all the good her late easy life
had done her seemed to have disappeared;
and from shame at her husband's conduct,
though her voice remained bright and shrill,
she did not dare to meet my eyes. I went

round to her, and held one of her thin work-worn hands as I spoke to her husband.

'And you've persuaded him that I'm not an ogre after all,' I said cheerfully.

Mr. Ellmer, after one or two vain attempts to answer, got back voice enough to whisper huskily, with a dogged expression of face—

'She says I was wrong—that if Babiole was unhappy, it was the fault of—the other one. Well, if I was wrong then, I'm right now. You'll marry her?'

'Yes.'

He gave a nod of satisfaction, and looked contemptuously at his wife.

'And she says I was mad! Perhaps so. But I was mad to some purpose if I shot the right man.'

With a hoarse weak laugh he turned away, and as she could not induce him to speak to me again, I bade him good-night and held out my hand, which, after a minute's consideration,

he took and even pressed limply for a moment
in his hot fingers.   I had scarcely got to the
door when his wife began to scold him for his
ingratitude, and he startled us both by suddenly finding voice enough to call me back.
He had struggled up on to his elbow, and a
rush of excitement had given him back his
strength for a few moments.

'She shall hold her tongue!' he growled
angrily, by way of prelude, as I returned to
the bedside.   'By your own showing you have
loved Babiole seven years?'

'Yes.'

'And during these long walks I have
watched you take with her lately on Craigendarroch and through the forest, you have
never told her so?'

'Never.   One can't be a man seven
years to be a scoundrel the eighth, Mr.
Ellmer.'

'Then which of us two ought to be the

most grateful now, I for your lending me a
roof to die under, or you for my bringing
back to you the woman you were a fool to
let go before.'

It was an impossible question for me to
answer, and I was thankful that the dying
man's ears caught the sound of footsteps on
the stairs, which diverted his attention from
me and gave me an opportunity to escape.
Outside the door I met Babiole, who flitted
past me quickly as I went down. I saw
no more of the ladies that night, for both
stayed at the cottage. But next day when
Ferguson came to my room, he informed
me that the poor fugitive had died early that
morning.

I was sincerely thankful that the unfortu-
nate man had slipped so easily out of the
chain of troubles he had forged for himself,
since, as I expected, intelligence of the affair
had already got abroad, and two police officers

from Aberdeen came down early in the afternoon, and were followed soon after by an official of the asylum from which Ellmer had made his escape.

Then there were inquiries to be held, and a great deal of elaborate fuss and formality to be gone through before the bodies of my poor friend and his crazy assailant could be laid quietly to rest. I sent the two widowed ladies away to Scarborough to recover from the effects of the torturing interrogatories of high - dried Scotch functionaries and gave myself up to a week of the most dismal wretchedness I ever remember to have endured, until the half-dozen judicial individuals who questioned me at various times and in various ways concerning details, of most of which I was entirely ignorant, succeeded in reducing me to a state of abject imbecility in which I answered whatever they pleased, and went very near to implicating myself in

the double catastrophe which was the subject
of the inquiry. A tragic occurrence must
always have for the commonplace mind an
element of mystery; if that element is not
afforded by the circumstances of the case, it
must be introduced by conjecture and ingenious cross-questioning of witnesses. Therefore, when at last the 'inquiry' was ended,
and victim and assailant were both buried in
Glenmuick churchyard amid the stolid interest of a little crowd of Highland women
and children, I found that I had become the
object of a morbid curiosity and horror as
the central figure of what had already become
a very ugly story.

I suppose that Fabian's death, the terrible
circumstances which surrounded it, and the
barrier they formed between myself and
Babiole, combined to make me more sensitive than of old. It is certain that popular
opinion, about which I had never before

cared one straw, now began to affect me strangely ; that my solitude became loneliness, and although the old wander-fever burned in me no longer, I began to feel that the mountains oppressed me, and the prospect of being snowed up with my books and my beasts, as I had been many times before, lowered in my horizon like a fear of imprisonment. I had heard nothing from Babiole except through her mother, whose letters were filled with minute accounts of the paralysing effect her husband's death seemed to have had upon the younger lady. These tidings struck me with dismay ! I began to feel that I had underestimated the effect that such a shock would have on a keenly sensitive nature, and to fear that his tragic death had perhaps done more to reinstate Fabian in the place he had first held in her heart than years of penitent devotion could have done. This conjecture became almost conviction when, just as I had found a pretext on which to visit the ladies, I received a letter from Babiole herself which struck all my hopes and plans to the ground. It was written in such a constrained manner that the carefully-chosen expressions of gratitude and affection sounded cold and formal; while the purport of the letter stood out as precise and clear as a sentence of death to me. She was going away. She found it impossible to impose longer upon my generosity, and she had obtained the situation of companion to a lady who was going to Algeria, and before the letter announcing the fact was in my hands, she would be on her way to France.

I confess I could have taken more calmly the burial of Larkhall and all it contained under an avalanche. That she could go like that, with no farewell but those few chilling words, on a journey, to an engagement to which she had bound herself, so she said, for three years, was a shock so great that it stunned me. To-to and Ta-ta both knew that night there was something wrong, and we sat, three speechless beasts, dolefully round the fire, without a rag of comfort between the lot of us. There was no use in writing; she was gone; besides, I wasn't quite a serf, and if she had no more feeling than that for me now that she was free, well at least she should not know that I was less philosophical. So I doggedly resolved to give up all thoughts of roaming, lest my ill-disciplined feet should carry me where I was not wanted; and, presenting a respectful but firm refusal to give up my lease of Larkhall to a certain great personage who had taken a fancy to it, I wrote a stupid letter to Mrs. Ellmer highly applauding her daughter's action, and settled myself down again to the bachelor life nature seems to have determined me for.

But the winds blow more coldly than they used to do across the bleak moors, the mists are more chilling than they used to be, and the broad lines of snow on Lochnagar, that I once thought such a pretty sight in the winter sun, look to me now like the pale fingers of a dead hand stretching down the mountain side, the taper points lengthening towards me day by day, even as the keen and nipping touch of a premature old age seems to threaten me as the new year creeps on and the zest of life still seems dead, and like a foolish woman who neglects the pleasures within her reach to dream idly of those she cannot have, I sneak through the deserted rooms of the old cottage when the sinking of the sun has allowed me to be maudlin without loss of self-respect, and I won't answer for it that I don't see ghosts in the silent rooms. And after all, what right has a man of nearly forty, and not even a decent-looking one at

that, to ask for better company ?   Poor little
witch !   Let her wake up to love and happiness with whom she will, after the feverish
dream of disappointed hope which I unwittingly encouraged, I'll not blame her, and it
will go hard with me, but I'll bring a cheerful
face to her second wedding   For a first love
which has not burnt itself out, but has been
extinguished at its height, leaves an inflam-
mable substance very ready to ignite again on
the earliest reasonable provocation.   And as
for me, I have To-to, Ta-ta, my books and my
pine-woods, and may be the spring will bring
me a better philosophy.

.   .   .   .   .

April.

P.S.—Spring has done it !   Surely never
was such a spring since the hawthorn buds
first burst on the hedges, and the pale green
tips of the hart's-tongue first peeped out of

the fissures in the gray rocks by the Gairn.
It all came at once too—sweet air and sun-
shine, and fresh bright green in the dark fringe
of the larches. Yesterday I swear we were
in the depths of as black and hard a winter as
ever killed the sheep in their pens, and split-
ting the earth with frost, caused great slabs
of rock to fall from their place on Craigendarroch into the pass below ; but this morning
came Babiole's letter, and when I went out of
the house with that little sheet of paper against
my breast, I found that it was spring. She
is back in England ; she 'would be glad to
see me' ; she 'hopes I shall soon find some
business to take me to London.' I rather
think I shall ; my portmanteau is packed indeed, my sandwiches are cut, the horse being
harnessed. And I haven't a fear for the end
now ; the embers are warm in her heart for
me, *me* to set glowing. The great personage
may have the lease of Larkhall at her pleasure ;

To-to and Ta-ta, and the rest of my small household must follow me to a warmer home in the South. For my exile is over, and I am reconciled to my kind.

Babiole wants me ; God bless her !

THE END

G. C. & Co.

Printed by R. & R. CLARK, *Edinburgh*

www.ingramcontent.com/pod-product-compliance
Lightning Source LLC
Chambersburg PA
CBHW020844020726
47497CB00005B/1245